TEN-EIGHTY

TEN-EIGHTY

ALLAN DAVIS

IGUANA

Copyright © 2023 Allan Davis
Published by Iguana Books
720 Bathurst Street, Suite 410
Toronto, ON M5S 2R4

Publisher: Cheryl Hawley
Editor: Toby Keymer
Front cover design: Ruth Dwight, designplayground.ca
Cover images: van photo by Zachary Keimig on Unsplash

ISBN 978-1-77180-598-8 (paperback)
ISBN 978-1-77180-597-1 (epub)

This is an original print edition of *Ten-Eighty*.

Other books in the Discards Series

Discards

From Muddy Water

Beyond the Headlights

Goodnight, Mr. Knight

CHAPTER ONE

Katria never thought about cemeteries or about the dead people lying in boxes six feet under until, on her fourteenth birthday, March 5, 2022, coming home from watching one of those *Undead* movies with her older sister, Renata, they got delayed by a funeral. They stood at the traffic light eating the rest of their popcorn and watched the hearse and the black flags flap the cars through red to yellow to green like a parade to the cemetery gate.

Renata said, "First they drain the blood and then they stuff the mouth with cotton and then they, like, open the windows before they stuff the butthole and then, hello hello, stuff that hole too."

Katria said, "Yeah. Totally."

...

It was the rhubarb growing along the back fence of their father's manicured lawn that got him started on his diet books. If he accidentally stepped on a rhubarb stalk, it didn't bother the rhubarb. It would grow up tall and straight the next day. If he accidentally ran over it with his brand-new Troy-Bilt XP lawnmower, canvas cover included, it didn't bother the rhubarb. The next day it would sprout up again and start to grow again and stand up straight again. He could cut it to pieces with the ax he had sharpened every spring, whether he had used it or not, and the rhubarb would grow back.

His diet books didn't have recipes for turning the stiff, straight stalks into pie or jam or pudding or squares, lots of sugar added, like a normal person's recipe book. His recipes turned rhubarb into strings of slimy stuff to be served with organic yogurt. His recipes turned rhubarb into a red sauce to spread over organic vegetables. His recipes turned rhubarb into a reddish gravy for lean organic free-range grass-fed meat.

Renata stared down at her plate of Dr. Ivan Boscov's No-Stroke Healthy Heart Through Rhubarb dinner and said, "It looks like my period."

And refused to eat it.

Katria said, "Yeah, totally."

And refused to eat it.

Not so for the people who bought the books. They ate the rhubarb and turned from sick to healthy. They ate the rhubarb and turned from fat to thin. They ate the rhubarb and turned from old to young. But then, oh my gosh, Katria hid the newspaper, March 6, 2022, under her mattress the day it got published, oh my gosh, just when her father was getting ready to go on the road selling his diet book, the *Toronto Sun* printed a picture of Sarah, his two-hundred-pound wife, Katria and Renata's two-hundred-pound mother, wolfing down Boston Creams in Tim Hortons.

One week later, Sarah died from a stroke. There was no funeral and no cemetery parade and no hearse and no black flags flapping the cars through red to yellow to green to the cemetery gate.

Katria said, "I don't get it, Renata. Why no funeral? And why won't our own father, Comrade Ivan, tell his own two daughters where their own mother is buried?"

Before Renata could answer, Comrade Ivan said, "We will have no more talk of your mother. She's disgraced me."

He said this as he was ripping up her death certificate. Katria intended to pick those pieces out of the garbage and Scotch tape them back together and hide the proof of death under her mattress. But Comrade Ivan used them like a collage pattern for the front and back covers of his next diet book: *Dr. Ivan Boscov's No-Stroke Healthy Heart: Leaner and Cleaner Through Rhubarb.*

...

Katria was standing at her bedroom window watching Comrade Ivan spraying his grass with pesticides. While he sprayed, he whistled and hummed a marching tune; she could hear it all the way up to her ears, like he was waving those little black cemetery flags for the little creatures soon to curl up comatose dead under his steel-toed boots.

When he finished spraying, he covered and tucked away his XP Sprayer in his garden shed. Then he unfolded his lawn chair from its hook on the right side behind the door and he sat admiring the flowers growing next to his rhubarb patch. He looked like he was deciding which to pick and wrap in green paper to take to Sarah, who, as far as Katria was concerned, did not die of a stroke on March 13, 2022, a week after Katria's fourteenth birthday, but was poisoned.

CHAPTER TWO

The word "dead" written in that jumble of letters on the diet book's cover was not like the word "dead" written in Katria's brain. Dead according to the law was not dead according to heart. Dead in some cemetery too far away to find was not dead in the cemetery close to her thoughts.

"Every time I look at the book cover, I get the feeling she's not, like, really dead."

Renata said, "Moms is dead. Grow up."

Renata said, "Moms was married to Ivan. Which means Moms has gone to a better place."

Renata said, "He didn't poison her; she had a stroke."

Katria said, "In those zombie movies the undead who walk the cemetery lanes barefoot with black toenails talk to the spirits of the real dead buried down below. I found this picture in Nana's storage room. See how much me and Moms look alike? I could almost pass for her. When I look at myself in the mirror, I think it's Moms come back from the undead."

Renata said, "Moms is dead. Get over it."

Katria began to notice that her thinking about the dead during the day and her thinking about the dead during the night were two different kinds of thinking. In her daytime thinking, she knew her mother was legally dead. But in her nighttime thinking, Katria began wondering if a living person, like herself, could make a connection with someone who seemed both not alive and not dead, like her mother. Katria began to think of Alexander Graham Bell from grade nine science class; if he could, with two tin cans and a length of wire, talk to his buddy in a room nearby, maybe she could, by using an umbilical spirit wire, talk to her mother in a cemetery nearby, if she knew which one.

Katria told Comrade Ivan, "I'm fourteen years old. I have a right to know. Where's the cemetery?"

A strange look came into Ivan's eyes. He said, "Whatever is buried must stay buried, gone for good."

Katria knew what was happening: Cover up, he might as well have said. Yes, I poisoned her for ruining the sales of my diet books.

Katria learned from studying the *Undead* movies that, if no one cared about the dead when they were alive, and no one cared about the dead when they were dead, then no one would ever come through the cemetery gate to visit their graves, which meant no one would ever try to make a connection with the dead on, say, Thanksgiving or Easter, or any other day. That was why they were the undead; they were waiting for their visitors, like, for example, Moms was waiting for her two daughters. Well, maybe not Renata, but for sure Katria.

In her bedroom in the dark of night, Katria imagined her mother drifting and wandering with the undead among the tombstones of this unknown cemetery. In the dim light of early morning, Katria could hear the mournful moanings of her mother mingled with the hollow wailings of the other undead walking with blackened toenails the cemetery lanes, midnight to dawn, waiting for their visitors.

But although during the night Katria felt chills and shivers up and down her spine and heard whispers and sighs in her head as she stared into the mirror at midnight trying to make a spirit umbilical hook-up through the glass, like a virtual visit on her laptop with someone who'd stepped off the map but was still somewhere close by, she never felt any actual connection, at least not like the undead with the not-dead in the *Living Dead* movies.

Renata said, "All the midnight noises you're hearing are caused by the wind in the trees and shit like that, know what I'm saying?"

Renata said, "And the creaking in the attic ... And yeah, maybe stray cats in the bushes. Know what I'm saying?"

...

As Katria watched Comrade Ivan step by step sweep his spray of poison brew back to front across the lawn, she imagined the little creatures beneath the fall of his steel-toed boots curling up dead the minute he passed. She imagined his poison percolating through the soil and traveling underground to the roots of rhubarb stalks that he had made Moms eat in large quantities to try to make her lose weight. Then, Katria could hardly believe it, the voice she heard sat her straight up in bed, almost like a down-on-her-knees vision, for from somewhere came the words of her mother: "It wasn't a stroke."

CHAPTER THREE

Renata Boscov's Cutting Corner Hair Salon, situated in downtown Toronto at Church and Carlton, drew a mix of clients: upscale business types, university kids, and a few from Regent Park public housing. The shop was narrow. The mirrors on two long walls reflected three leather chairs in a row and, at the back, one sink with a shampoo chair.

Renata's five o'clock customer for the third of May was an older lady for a perm: Mrs. Rawson, who had a Regent Park address. Not one of Renata's regulars.

Mrs. Rawlins was short and stout with a double chin that jiggled as she struggled to ease her ample self into the shampoo chair. Mrs. Rawlins settled herself while Renata turned on the water, tested it for temperature, and then tipped Mrs. Rawlins's head back for the gentle wash, at the same time inspecting the scalp for any sores that might be irritated by perm products. The hair, a natural grey, was a bit too thin for a good curl, which meant a perm was not a good idea. It didn't suit her age either, but … what the lady wants, the lady gets.

Renata finished the rinse, and Mrs. Rawlins pulled herself upright.

Mrs. Rawlins said, "You look too young to give a decent perm." Her voice was hard and raspy.

A smoker, thought Renata, as she wrapped the towel around the damp hair.

"I'm twenty-two. I've been a hairdresser for five years. I know what I'm doing." But don't blame me if you don't like it, she wanted to add, your hair strands are too thin.

Renata helped her from the shampoo station to the chair nearest the door. In the mirrors, Renata noticed the lady scowling at her doubtfully, sizing up Renata's tight jeans, her sleeveless top, her blonde hair pulled back in a ponytail. This was her standard uniform most days, although each day she wore a different style of jeans and a different top.

Mrs. Rawlins pointed. "I see you're well prepared. You've got all your stuff ready. Like a dentist."

"I'm well prepared, everything I need, like a dentist, yes."

"Every time I get a perm, my husband calls me The Poodle. He says I look more loopy than usual. Poodles are lovable and cute and intelligent, I say. 'Unlike you,' he says."

Renata said, "When I was little, my aunt Gizla, she called my sister and me Dearie because she couldn't remember our names or which one was which. Sometimes she called me Emma, who's my half-sister from my father's first marriage. My nana was the same. They each had a poodle called Rolfie and they each had a goldfish called Dr. Goldstein. Nana got mentally bent from hiding out in a storage room in Moscow until the war ended. Nana passed her bentness on to her daughter, my aunt Gizla. So, when they moved to this country they each got a one-bed apartment with a walk-in closet they called the storage room. They babysat us a lot, you know, either we were at Nana's or Aunt Gizla's, and, if we were bad, we'd be locked in the storage room."

"I think that's called abuse."

"Yeah, totally. But you know, from the war." Renata fiddled with the smock, making certain it would prevent any product from running down into Mrs. Rawlins's dress, not all that easy, like covering a cruise ship with Saran wrap.

"My daughter told me don't get a perm if you're in menopause because your hormones are going haywire, and your hair will end up looking like haywire."

"You'll like the perm," Renata assured her, "but I can't do much about your menopause."

"My husband calls menopause Mad Cow Disease."

Ha ha. You're a funny old bitch, Mrs. Rawlins. Renata slipped one latex glove onto her left hand. She began to part the hair into three sections, one down the middle and two on each side. In the mirror, Renata caught Mrs. Rawlins giving her the up and down.

"If I had your looks, I wouldn't need a perm. And your figure. You look like Marilyn Monroe. Well, she was before your time. You've already won the birth lottery. What did you say your name was?"

"Renata."

"Don't make me look like a goddamn poodle, Renata. I don't want to get killed by that dog poisoner."

"The dog poisoner, yeah. Totally."

"He's becoming a bit of a hero, you know. Everyone hates pit bulls and Rottweilers and Dobermans. And those little yappers are all over the place. But the dog poisoner isn't bothering with the little ones. Do you know why? He's being paid by the pound."

Ha ha. You're a funny old bitch, Mrs. Rawlins. Renata said, "You're not going to look like a poodle."

"I listened to a radio program. A woman phoned in to say a man moved in down the street with a wolf-dog. That's what it looked like, she said. It weighed about a hundred pounds. She was coming along the sidewalk from the 7-Eleven with a bag of chips and this wolf-dog lunged at the chips and ripped them out of her hand. The man dragged off the dog and gave her five dollars for the chips, which the dog was eating, bag and all. So, she told a friend who gave her a phone number, and a week later that dog was dead."

Renata paused to flex her fingers, which today were feeling a little stiff. "I guess that's why the dog poisoner is a hero."

"I heard of another lady who was terrorized by the black Lab next door. It would jump over the fence and gallop around and knock her over. While she was digging in the flower garden, it would grab her hand, leaving teeth marks, so she'd go inside, leaving it out there trampling the flowers while she phoned the owner who'd say, 'Oh he's just a pup, just being playful.' So the lady phoned the police and they said for her to build a better fence."

"Yeah. Totally. The police don't do anything."

"I saw a news interview with the Humane Society. The reporter asked what's the most common dog complaint. So the Humane Society man says, 'Barking.' So the reporter says, 'What should people do about that instead of hiring the dog poisoner?' So the Humane Society man says, 'Hire a burglar. Give the dog a reason to bark.'"

"Yeah, totally. No one is taking the dog complaints seriously. But I'm taking your perm seriously. You're going to look lovely."

"As well as being young and pretty, you're a good liar. There are good liars and bad liars. The prisons are full of bad liars, the churches are full of good liars. But you don't look like you go to church and you don't look like you've been in prison."

"I've been to church but not to prison."

"My husband says, 'Here's what I learned in church: You got to try and make the best of not much. That's why I married a poodle.'"

"You're not going to look like a poodle."

Renata wound another curler and glanced at Mrs. Rawlins, who was still watching her in the mirror. "You always dress this way, Renata?"

She shrugged. "Just jeans and a top."

"You've got a nice ass in those tight jeans, and with those two moneymakers you got trying to break out of that of that tank top you could bed the president. Marilyn Monroe proved it. She said women have all the power because women have all the vaginas."

"I guess."

"So along comes some rich guy, like in that movie *Pretty Woman*, and he leaves you all his money."

"Yeah, totally. I could sure use it."

"Then you could spend all day walking around in a miniskirt with your poodle, like Paris Hilton."

Renata finished the perm, ran Mrs. Rawlin's card, closed the shop, and went home. She right away got on Google. Up came a newspaper item under "Rash of Dog Poisonings." She fixed herself a vodka and sat on the chesterfield. She learned that the victims were all attack dogs living in upper-crust Rosedale and Forest Hill. According to the article, the dog poisoner was thought to be working for a home burglary gang disabling security systems that used dogs instead of electronics. Renata felt relieved. She knew Comrade Ivan needed money to promote his diet books. But there was no way he'd be involved in home invasion robberies.

CHAPTER FOUR

Katria had decided that now that she was fourteen and a half, she was old enough to sneak off on her own whenever she wanted, out the back door, cut through the rhubarb patch, over the fence, up two blocks to Mount Hope Cemetery, where that parade had ended. It wasn't by chance that her life had been interrupted by that parade. But, if she didn't find Moms there, then she would go up ten blocks, over twenty blocks, whatever it took, and into each cemetery one by one to hike the lanes backward in time to find Moms, whose last name was Boscov, the same as hers, and who, Katria had learned from searching "ancestry" on the net, she'd find out all about if she bought the Deluxe Search Software for ninety-nine dollars. She didn't have ninety-nine dollars, but she had subway fare to go wherever she wanted.

Katria imagined the cemetery lanes as streets and the tombstones as houses, each with a name. On one of these, she'd see "Boscov." Then she'd see the first name, "Sarah." Then she'd knock on the door, and the door would be answered, and she'd ask Moms all those questions she needed to find answers for, like for example, did Comrade Ivan kill her because she got her picture taken in Tim Hortons and made him look like the phoney he was? Katria would ask her that one. And another one. Did Comrade Ivan kill her with the same poison he used on the lawn? And another one that she thought might be more likely: did he kill her with the same poison he used to kill those dogs?

Renata said, "Nah. He's not the dog poisoner. A customer of mine, Mrs. Rawlins, heard on the news that it's probably a postal worker. Thousands are bitten every year, some seriously. One postman they interviewed said when he pepper-sprayed a pit bull that was attacking him he was beaten up by the dog's owner. Another said he used plastic tongs to put letters through the mail slot for fear of being bitten by the dog waiting on the other side. One postal worker said he felt like filling an envelope full of poison and shoving it through the mail slot, that's how pissed he was."

Rain or shine, Katria tracked the Mt. Hope Cemetery lanes, each one ending in the back corner at the grave of Mary McCraney. At least it seemed to end that way because that's where she always stopped to sit down in the grass with a plunk like her mother, not cross-legged like those meditation guys, easy for them because they were skinny, and Katria, from eating nothing but day-old donuts she got free from Tim Hortons instead of that rhubarb crap, was getting heavy stove-pipe legs like Moms, and that was her intention.

McCraney was a Scottish name, so Mary was Scottish, like Katria's mother. Mary McCraney had been fifteen. Mary McCraney was lying six feet below, still wearing her neat white dress and blue socks and plain black shoes, shiny and clean, new maybe, never been walked in on the stony ground of the laneway that got her here, no dust on them, never been wet with rain. That's where rain comes from, Katria said to Dead Mary, all the children left abandoned, crying for their undead mothers, and all the undead mothers right now crying for their not dead children.

Katria wanted Dead Mary to ask undead Moms some questions, a lot more questions than before, now that she was thinking about rain being tears. And she had a lot of other related questions she should've asked while her mother was alive, like for example: Does she remember laying me down in my bassinette, tucking me in, giving me a soother? Does she remember that? Did she imagine me growing up to be somebody, like a nurse or a teacher? Ask her that. Ask her something else. Ask her whether I did anything bad when I was little. Ask her that, because I don't remember. Whatever it was I did, I'm sorry.

Katria got invited by Renata to come over to see her new apartment on Sherbourne and to have a serious talk. Unusual for Renata, who was never serious about anything. Katria was expecting some crap from Facebook like, "The door that gets closed on the worst thing that can happen to any kid, namely the loss of the most important person in their life, namely the mother, should stay closed no matter how many times the kid knocks, blah, blah, blah."

And Katria would shrug and say, "Yeah, well, I guess. Yeah, totally."

What Renata actually said was, "You should be hanging out with other kids, not sitting in the grass and the weeds like Crazy Person talking to Dead Person, know what I'm saying?"

Mary McCraney was no chatterbox, that's for sure, so even if Mary McCraney had asked Moms the questions, Katria probably wouldn't get much of an answer.

CHAPTER FIVE

Every morning the wrinkles and the frowns in Emma Boscov's bathroom mirror reminded her that she was thirty-eight and that each day was bringing her closer to a life of loveless spinsterhood.

But, said Emma to Emma in the mirror, at only thirty-eight, I'm still attractive enough. I still have that girl-next-door look.

I know, said the mirror. The girl next door in you is what keeps you in the doorway, too shy to step out and meet someone. So, if single is your fate, you need to guarantee your future. You have no pension plan, no investments, but you have saved the money inherited from your mother.

These words from Emma-in-the-mirror were in her thoughts when her employer for the past twelve years mentioned selling the Flower Shoppe. This was like Emma in Wonderland, either stepping into the mirror, or stepping out of it. Emma signed for the bank loan on the first of July. The sign in the front window now read: "Emma's Flowers. Banquets, Weddings, Funerals, Birthdays. Free Delivery, Open 7 Days a Week, 9 to 9."

The sign did not read: "I'm in debt up to my ears, business has been so slow, I can't afford to pay my landlord back-rent on my apartment, and I'm going to end up sleeping with my flowers in my car."

As Emma was finishing her lunch at the back of the store, a tall, broad-shouldered, trim-waisted man stepped in. Emma hadn't seen him in ten years and she did not want to see him now.

Emma said, "I have no interest in talking to you. But I'll give you flowers for Sarah's grave. If you're here for anything else, you should just leave."

Her father looked startled. "How did you know she died?"

"Renata phoned me with the news. I hadn't talked to her or Sarah in ten years."

He looked apologetic, unusual for a man who had drilled into Emma's head his Russian moto: Never apologize to anyone.

He said, "I'm here about your sister. Katria."

"Half-sister."

The shop door opened. Ivan glanced at the two ladies who had stepped in. "But we can't talk here. Will you meet me for dinner this evening?"

. . .

Ivan, wearing a suit and tie, arrived at the expensive Italian restaurant with two books under his arm. "I brought you a copy of each of my diet books."

Emma leafed through the pages as she sipped her wine.

"*Dr.* Boscov? You're a medical doctor now?"

"My nutrition practice is a sideline. But since my Ph.D. from the University of Moscow says doctor, I can call myself Doctor."

Emma snorted. "In engineering. Not medicine. So why are you into a diet book scam? The last time I saw you, you had your own engineering company."

"Your mother took half when she divorced me. But even before that, the company wasn't doing well. I had to learn the hard way that things are done differently here. In Russia, we fix things: bridges with cracks, towers that lean, roofs that sag. It's called repurposing. Here in North America, they tear things down. It's called depurposing. My expertise is in correcting the engineering mistakes of others. The structures here that would usually be saved in Russia end up in North American demolition. So, as well as the diet books, I have had to take on another sideline business."

He handed her his business card:

GUARANTEED GONE

Rodent Removal Consultant

"When a building is torn down, the rats, bats, raccoons, squirrels, whatever is in there, go searching for a new place to live. They find their way into other buildings through cracks in the foundations, holes in the soffits, sags in the roof. Raccoons, for example. First, I have one of my men smoke them out. Then I have one of my men correct the cracks and the holes and the sags, in other words, all the entry points. For anything left inside, rats, for example, I have one of my men lay out the poison."

Emma noted that the picture on the card was a white van, unmarked except for two crossed knitting needles on the side, the same symbol as was on the front of the card.

Emma said, "I sell flowers. I don't sell diet books, if that's why you're here, and I don't have need of your extermination services, although I'm sure you're good at it."

He put on his phoney apologetic look. "I'm not here about that. I need help with Katria. She won't talk to me or Aunt Gizla or Nana. Renata comes and goes but is not a good influence. All I am asking is that you come over and talk to her."

"She was four years old when I left. She won't know me."

"That is why I am asking. As an absentee half-sister, your connection with Katria hasn't been ruined yet."

Emma felt her memory reboot itself to the times she was locked in that storage closet by Aunt Gizla, or Nana, so they could watch the TV knitting show in peace. "I want nothing to do with the Russian Boscovs."

"Please, Emma? I need your help. So what can I do for you in return for it?"

Emma was thinking, yesterday had been brisk for the first hour and then business had faded into nothing. The flowers she had bought that morning ended up in the green bin that night.

"How about an interest-free loan of ten thousand dollars that I pay back when I feel like it?"

...

A few days later Emma drove to her father's address, a newish two-story with a manicured front lawn bordered on either side by a flawlessly trimmed hedge. Katria was inside, sprawled on the chesterfield in the perfectly tidy living room. Dressed in heavy grey tracks pants, multiple unmatched sweaters, and a winter coat, even though it was a hot summer day, she looked like a teenage bag lady come in out of the cold. This girl, who had been a four-year-old cutie when Emma left, was now an overweight, vacant-eyed fourteen-year-old with the deathly whitish-grey complexion of a corpse.

In the opposite matching chair sat Renata, thirteen when Emma left, now a knock-out twenty-two: long-legged, blonde, and sexy in her mini-skirt and spaghetti-strap top.

Renata got up and came over to give Emma a warm hug. "Welcome to the Russian Front."

Katria disappeared up the stairs.

Renata made coffee.

As Emma poured the milk from the carton and dished the sugar from the sugar bowl, she said, "What in the world is going on with Katria?"

Renata set down her cup across from Emma at the kitchen table. "She stays in her room and refuses to eat anything but Tim Hortons donuts and refuses to talk to anyone except her pet mouse, Algernon, from that story where the lab mouse is smarter than the man, Charlie."

As Emma watched Renata add the milk and sugar, Emma remembered, she could hear Ivan saying it, you can't serve the milk from the carton and you should be using the little coffee spoons and don't slouch and no TV until you've done your homework and no sleepovers until you've cleaned up your room and on and on, sparks in the gunpowder.

Renata set down her spoon. "Have you read his diet books? Guess not. Well, he's got this thing about rhubarb, you know, it prevents cancer, keeps your heart healthy, all that antioxidant stuff."

Emma sipped her coffee and waited for Renata to continue.

"Yeah, well, Sarah was overweight. She ate a lot of junk food, mostly donuts, so he put her on his stupid rhubarb diet. Sarah tried to lose weight, but all that rhubarb made her sick. When she died from a stroke, Katria decided the poison he sprayed on his lawn got into the rhubarb growing along the fence and got into the rhubarb he was making Moms eat and that gave her a stroke. So now Katria eats nothing but donuts, and says she won't stop until she reaches two hundred pounds, which is what Moms weighed when he killed her."

"And then what? When she reaches two hundred pounds, then what?"

Renata shrugged. "I think that's why Ivan asked you to come. We don't know then what."

"Am I missing something? How does any of this make sense?"

"Since when did anything ever make sense in this family?"

Emma stirred her coffee, tasted it, and added more sugar. "Why didn't Sarah tell him where to shove his rhubarb?"

Renata seemed puzzled. "What? Have you forgotten what Ivan is like? Sarah was a plain Scottish girl. She couldn't stick up for herself. Ivan is Ivan."

"But it's obvious that Katria is getting dietary deficiency problems and needs to see a doctor."

"She refuses to go, and he can't make her go."

While Renata made another pot of coffee, Emma took a tour of the house. The rooms were furnished with various pieces of Russian furniture made from walnut. At least, that's what Ivan would say. Emma didn't know much about furniture. It could've been from

Walmart. The upstairs bathroom was small but recently remodelled, it looked like, no doubt by Ivan, as was the downstairs bathroom, as was the back deck overlooking the perfectly manicured, lush, and green back lawn. Emma was a florist. She knew this lawn came from the twilight zone of pesticide, herbicide, and artificial fertilizer treatments spring, summer, and fall using twilight zone chemicals that had been banned years ago: Armageddon for butterflies, moths, caterpillars, flying bugs, walking bugs, crawling bugs, dew worms, ants; no bug in this top-to-bottom insect chain survived DDT.

Emma began to wonder. She wondered if he used banned poison from Russia to kill the rats and the raccoons and the squirrels and whatever else he killed. She wondered about the crossed knitting needles symbol, as sinister a sign as a swastika. Emma remembered that Nana had won so many sets of ebony knitting needles in various contests that she gave some to him. He kept them in his desk drawer. After work he'd take them out and hold them, usually shifting them from one hand to the other, as though he thought there should be a left and a right. To Emma they looked identical, perfectly straight and perfectly matched, gleaming identical glints in the overhead light as his brow furrowed in crooked lines and the edges of his mouth turned down in a mismatched frown as he arranged them in geometric patterns on the surface of his desk. She had thought, well, he's an engineer. That's how his mind works, level and square, which was why he had the habit of straightening the pictures on the wall, correcting the overhang sag of the bedspread, and smoothing away wrinkles in the sheets. He especially disliked wrinkles. Emma guessed it was because wrinkles were never straight nor square, no matter how hard you tried to smooth them geometrically flat.

Emma remembered the high-powered juice and vegetable drinks that he'd mix up with raw eggs in a high-powered blender and drink while he ate his high-powered oatmeal with a stewed fruit mix that looked like brown algae.

Emma's mother, Ivan's first wife, would say, "For breakfast I have Shreddies."

"Shreddies are 90% sugar."

Emma's mother would say, "For lunch, I have a can of soup and a ham sandwich."

"Processed ham is full of chemicals. Canned soup is high in salt."

Emma's mother finally said, "I usually have no interest in your epic correctness, except today I do. These divorce papers are epically correct."

Emma did not want to come back to that. But neither did she want to lose her flower shop. And more importantly, she could not, could not, walk away from her baby sister, who in Emma's mind was still the four-year-old cutie.

Renata left after a second coffee but Emma waited for Ivan, who had said he'd be home by twelve. When he arrived, he placed on the kitchen table two new hardcover books: *Healthy Living Through Rhubarb* and *Leaner and Cleaner with Rhubarb*.

He said, "People think rhubarb is a fruit, but it's a vegetable. It's rich in magnesium, vitamin C, vitamin K, potassium, and fibre. For maximum health outcomes, it should be one-third of every plate."

Emma said, "Have you not yet figured out why Katria decided to get back at you by eating nothing but donuts?"

He did what he always did: pretended not to hear. He picked up the books and handed them to Emma. "Sales of both titles have been excellent. I have an interview coming up on CBC. I intend to give up the rodent control business and promote my books full time."

Emma was remembering, yesterday was brisk for the first hour and then business faded into nothing. The flowers she had bought that morning ended up in the green bin that night. "I'll give up my apartment and stay here and help Katria if you loan me ten thousand dollars, which I might repay if you treat me with respect while I'm here helping Katria. But if you expect me to cook anything with rhubarb, think again. I hate rhubarb. Farmers feed rhubarb to the pigs."

"I don't have ten thousand dollars."

"Your daughter or your money. Maybe for once in your life think about someone besides yourself."

CHAPTER SIX

The ten-thousand-dollar loan in the bank, Emma's furniture in storage, her clothes moved into Ivan's spare bedroom, Emma and Renata were celebrating sisters back together in Renata's downtown one-bed apartment. Renata had mixed two vodkas. "Remember? Russian tradition." Renata held up her glass. "Like back in the homeland before the communists."

Emma copied Renata's down the hatch and then said, "Ivan must be hard to work for in his rodent-killing business."

"He would be if he had anyone working for him. He works by himself."

"So why did he tell me he had all these employees?"

"Are you forgetting how he is? He's a bullshitter. He never wanted to be an exterminator, although he does seem to enjoy destroying planet Earth with his illegal poisons."

"I wondered about that. Where does he get them?"

Renata shrugged. "From Russia, I guess. Who knows? Probably stuff left over from the war."

"And where's Katria getting the money to buy those donuts? She's got bags of them in her bedroom."

"She doesn't need money. Instead of throwing out the day-olds, Tim Hortons gives them away. Bags full."

Emma said, "She needs to see a psychiatrist who will commit her."

"The waitlist is long, and besides, she'd refuse to go."

Emma watched Renata get up to mix two more drinks. "I noticed he grows monkshood in the back yard. Its roots are poisonous. Rhubarb leaves are poisonous. Yesterday evening when I came home from work, I watched him with his pesticide sprayer, bending down to watch the little creatures curl up and die. He's like a little boy pulling the legs off spiders. Did he kill Sarah?"

Renata's hesitation was suspicious, so when she said, "The answer is no. She was overweight. She had a stroke. Don't let Katria convince you otherwise," Emma was even more suspicious.

Emma began to make notes on Katria's daily routines. She stayed day and night in her room dressed in her mother's flannel PJs with her mother's bathrobe fastened up to her neck so that all that was visible of Katria was her grey-white face. She spent a lot of time staring into the mirror. Emma remembered how her mirror each day added another wrinkle. Katria's mirror each day seemed to add another pound. But Emma's mirror made her take steps to correct her situation. In Katria's case, instead of her mirror making her correct her situation and lose weight, it was making her gain weight by eating more Tim Hortons. It was like every time Katria looked in that mirror an arm came out of the glass and handed her another donut.

A week after she moved in, Emma invited Renata for a Sunday family dinner. Emma remembered Ivan's family dinners, usually spent listening to Ivan badgering Sarah about her weight while little Katria with big brown eyes watched and listened and often, not understanding, began to cry.

When Renata finally arrived at the front door, intentionally late, of course, Ivan, who had been keeping the food warm on hot plates, sat down at the head of the dining room table with Emma opposite him, taking Sarah's place. Renata took her place on one side, and then Katria sat on the other side. Ivan said grace. You had to be thankful for the rhubarb Ivan was about to feed you. Ivan scooped out Katria's portion. Proportion, he called it. Fish, brown rice, and something that looked like dandelion leaves in rhubarb sauce, and something else that looked like ketchup on toast.

He handed Katria a heaped plate. He said, "Have you ever heard of the useless eaters? That bit of history is probably not in the books you read in school. Herr Backe, a nice little man who went to the opera on Saturday and church on Sunday, was Nazi Germany's Minister of Agriculture. He invented the Hunger Plan, which was to invade Russia, seize all its agricultural land, and ship the food back to Germany. He called us Russians 'useless eaters.'"

"I'm only a florist," said Emma, "but I know Katria's problems are with the Russians not the Germans."

He unfolded his serviette. "That's because you don't know our family history. In the war Nana hid from the Germans in the storage room of their building all day and night, except when she snuck out for food. Nana told me stories that the Russian women would sleep with the German soldiers for food. To these women, the German soldiers looked like food, their fingers like sausages and their faces like apple pie."

Ivan glanced at Emma then turned to Katria. "So I'm telling you to be thankful you have food. During the Soviet famines, people ate their children."

Katria was staring into her steaming plate. "I'll eat this plate of poison if you tell me what kind of poison you used on my mother."

Knife in his left hand, fork in his right, Ivan did not up look up from his dinner. "She died of a stroke from being overweight and not eating properly."

"Renata's birthday is next week. I'll eat a plate full of Renata's birthday cake but I will not eat a plate of your poison."

Renata said, "I've seen pictures of the Russian grannies. They all look like they need to join Weight Warriors."

Emma said, "Mr. Google says rhubarb in large quantities is poisonous."

"Nonsense. Rhubarb has been used for its medicinal properties for centuries. Russian rhubarb was known as the best."

Katria was staring at her Sunday dinner that, Emma knew, Ivan had spent Sunday afternoon preparing. Then, using her fork, Katria shifted the rhubarb-sauced rice to one side of the plate, and then the dandelion leaves to the other side, and then the fish into the middle, dividing the plate into three. Then, using a knife and fork together, she began to pile the rice and the leaves onto the fish and stir them into a mushy paste with blobs of red like puke on a sidewalk.

Ivan said, "Do you know how, in the Second World War, the Russians identified the German spies? By inviting them to dinner. The Germans ate with their forks in the fists like they were shovelling. One of the few things that differentiate us from animals is we use cutlery and eat properly."

Emma watched Katria bend low over her plate and, elbows deep in slimy red sauce, shovel it in. If she'd been ambidextrous, she'd have used two spoons like shovels. Then she excused herself, got up, and went into the downstairs bathroom. They all sat listening to her puke it all up. Emma was certain that, after Katria was finished, because her mouth would taste like sewage, she would brush her teeth.

But Katria came straight out of the bathroom and sat at the table. She reached into her pocket for a package of gum. She brought the stick of gum to her mouth and began an open-mouth chew. She sat there chewing and snapping her gum. She said, "I eat nothing but donuts. I puke up your goddam Sunday thanks-for-what-we-are-about-to-receive dinner and I'm going to keep on doing it until you admit to me that you poisoned my mother."

She got up and disappeared upstairs.

Ivan threw up his hands. "You see, Emma? What am I supposed to do? Now she's up in her room playing with her mouse."

Emma, followed by Renata, pushed back her chair and went up the stairs and along the hall and tapped on Katria's bedroom door. They walked in and climbed onto the bed with her.

Emma asked, "How can you puke and not brush your teeth? I can't stand puke in my mouth. It tastes like poison."

"That's why I do it, to taste his poison."

Renata tapped Katria on the shoulder. "You aren't hurting him. You're only hurting yourself."

"I'm going to use some of his poison on him. See how he likes it."

"You can't do that, Katria."

"First, I'll poison Rolfie and then I'll poison Aunt Gizla and then I'll poison Nana and then I'll poison him."

"Why Rolfie?"

"When I used to go over to Aunt Gizla's, when I was like ten, and Rolfie started sniffing my crotch, Aunt Gizla would put me in the storge room. Aunt Gizla would say, Katria, go into the storage room so Rolfie can't do that."

Renata tapped her on the shoulder. "If you poison them, you'll go to jail."

"I'll use untraceable poison."

"There's no such thing. Maybe twenty years ago. But now forensics can trace anything."

CHAPTER SEVEN

When Emma Googled "untraceable poisons," up came a videotaped interview with a Dr. Chan who worked for the pharma company that had bought the Schneider's plant on Keele Street. The old meat packing buildings had been replaced by office buildings. Dr. Chan, a poison specialist, worked in the basement of the old Weiner Plant. He was standing before a cage of white rats.

"The only rat poisons available today are becoming ineffective. So, if selenium can be traced to an enzyme by an autopsy, it can be marketed as a rodenticide more effective than warfarin."

Emma recognized the CBC journalist, Scott something, a rough-looking character, balding and heavy, always scruffily dressed, his early morning face always more crumpled than his afternoon face. Scott said, "But more dangerous to pets, dogs, in particular. I'm referring to the rash of dog poisonings that has hit Toronto."

The camera shifted to a close-up of Dr. Chan. "Dogs will eat anything: discarded meds, antifreeze, whatever. Those are accidental poisonings. Most intentional dog poisoning can be traced to warfarin. But yes, in the last year, there have been a lot of suspected poisonings that can't be traced. Most of them young, healthy dogs in their prime. Yet their autopsies indicate the cause of death as strokes, which is highly unlikely."

Dr. Chan opened the cage and took out one rat and cradled it crouched in his palm. "That's the problem. Poisoning causes stroke-like symptoms. So, by discovering the enzyme that attacks the vital organs, I can trace the poison. If an autopsy can identify the poison, the police might be able to trace the poisoner. In theory, anyway." Dr. Chan smiled. "In my business, everything starts off as theory."

Emma remembered that Scott had been one of the first journalists to write articles dismissing the US claim that Iraq had chemical weapons. His famous line was, "There's nothing so powerful as the truth." He seemed to have a thing about poisons as weapons. He continued, "But even then, selenium would still be difficult to prosecute under the category of federal offense because selenium is commonly used in insecticides. In other words, something a dog might get into. Then an autopsy would say 'death by pulmonary edema caused by accidental poisoning by insecticides containing selenium.' So. We're no further ahead."

Dr. Chan gave a long sigh. "Well, yes. Depending on the food-to-poison ratio, the lingering and easily detectable smell emitted from the lungs and the pores of the skin due to the excretion of dimethyl selenide is traceable during the first hour after death. But it becomes more difficult to trace as the body settles into decomposition, which means if the autopsy isn't immediate, which it rarely is, and the individual doing the autopsy isn't looking for the enzyme, then a trace is unlikely, so, on and on it goes. Every answer has another question, which means you media guys will always have something to ask questions about."

"There's nothing so powerful as the truth." Scott smiled briefly, then continued, "Which leads me to the next question. We've been talking about dogs. What about people?"

Chan thought for a moment. With the tips of his fingers, he stroked his rat. "Autopsies for people are more thorough. And now that I've identified the enzyme, almost any dimwit coroner could put together enough evidence from tissue samples to get convictions for most selenium poisonings in people. But again, they would have to be looking for it and it would need to be in large quantities. For example, if a wife were feeding her husband low quantities of selenium, not enough to kill him quickly, but enough to do serious cell damage over time, the poison would not be easily traced and the cause of death would be ruled as heart failure."

While Dr. Chan talked, the camera lingered close up on the rat. Its little pink nose wiggling, its pink eyes stared at the back and forth pacing of its cage mates.

Scott continued. "How about another possibility: the poison called fluoroacetate, otherwise known as ten-eighty. From what I've read, ten-eighty is the best murder weapon on the market."

At the mention of ten-eighty the rat shifted and squirmed in Dr. Chan's hand. Its little nose seemed to be sniff-sniffing its coming execution by ten-eighty.

"If your wife asked me what the best way to put you down was, I'd recommend ten-eighty. It's so highly toxic, death results from an extremely small amount, leaving no evidence of poison. Except it's been banned almost everywhere, except for research purposes, and in some countries for use by government wildlife authorities."

With the tip of his finger Dr. Chan continued to stroke the rat, calming it down. "But like everything else that's been banned, you can get it in Canada on the black market, although with the border tightening up, it's becoming harder to sneak through. So yes, it could be the dog poisoner we're talking about has a black-market connection and is using ten-eighty, probably from Russia."

The camera followed Dr. Chan back to his desk. "Murder by poison happens more often than you might think. No proof, of course. A disgruntled wife poisons the husband, and the coroner rules it cardiac arrest, the wife walks."

Emma did not need to see more. She copied down the link for the Dr. Chan interview. Then she scrolled down and printed every article she could find on ten-eighty. Then Emma settled herself into the only comfortable chair in Ivan's perfect living room and made notes as she read:

- *Otherwise known as ten-eighty, a naturally occurring untraceable toxin found in plants throughout the world.*

- *In the 1940s it was manufactured into a sodium salt and sold as pest control. But it proved to be so highly toxic to mammals that only licensed pest control operators could use it.*

- *Water-soluble, no smell, no taste, easily mistaken as table salt, readily absorbed through the gastrointestinal tract into the vital organs, death by heart failure with no known antidote, so lethal that in 1972 the use of ten-eighty was banned in the U.S. for predator control. For rodenticide use, it was banned in 1985.*

CHAPTER EIGHT

Emma had an idea. Using glue and duct tape, she created a maze box, taking care to make no part of the maze box straight or square, with a crooked pretzel at the finish line. She walked unannounced into Katria's room and laid the unsquare box on Katria's bed. She lifted Algernon out of his cage and placed him at the start line, where he sat for a few seconds wig-wiggling his whiskers and sniffing the air. Then he set off through the crooked maze, up and down into blind alleys backward and forward along lopsided detours in a halting, erratic scramble to the pretzel.

When he had finished the pretzel, Katria added another pretzel, picked up the mouse, and again watched him run the erratic zigzag of the crooked pattern to the crooked pretzel.

Without asking permission, Emma settled herself down on Katria's bed and introduced herself. "Hello, Algernon. My name is Emma."

Algernon was busy eating his pretzel.

"A teacher came into my flower shop today with her grade three class. One of the students asked her how to spell chrysanthemum. The teacher didn't know. I said, 'I don't know how to spell it either, and I'm the florist.'"

Algernon looked like he was listening.

Emma said, "My mother told me you have two choices: either you make your life about flowers or about thistles. That's why I went into the flower business."

Katria said to Algernon, "My nana taught my father to look at the thistles in life. That's why he got into the poison business. Just sayin'."

Emma directed a question to Algernon: "Why exactly is Katria eating nothing but donuts? I know the explanation Renata has given. But I'd like to hear your thoughts. She likes you better than the rest of us, so I'm sure she's talked to you about it."

Katria said, "I read about this girl, her name was Georgie. All she ate was donuts. After five years, she looked about forty, although she was only eighteen. My mother died from his poison when she was forty. In a year or two, I'll look like my mother at forty. Ivan will say, 'Is this Katria, or is this the ghost of Sarah come back to kill me with my own poison?'"

Katria searched through the bottom drawer of her dresser and gave Emma a picture. Emma took it to the window for a closer look. It was a shoulder-up photo of Sarah at sixteen. Katria and Sarah could've been twins, so much alike it was spooky.

Emma came back to the bed and said to Algernon, "So, Katria is getting revenge for her mother by taking the place of her mother. 'Here I am, back to haunt you.' I have to admit, it's effective. It's like the ghost of Sarah has climbed out of her coffin and taken over Katria's body. It's Sarah, back from the dead. But, of course, Algernon, as you would expect, she's getting nutritional deficiency problems."

"It's going to be worth it, Emma."

Katria had given Emma hugs when she was four years old. Emma had given Katria hugs and pulled her up on her knee. So now it seemed natural to give Katria a hug. Emma didn't know how it happened but it must have seemed natural to Katria to climb up on Emma's knee because now Katria, without thinking, it seemed, had done just that.

...

Emma went to the bookstore and bought the book *Flowers for Algernon* and gave it to Algernon. The next day, Saturday, she brought home a tiny bouquet and put it beside Algernon's cage. Emma sat on the bed. Katria sat beside her. Katria considered the flowers. Then she lifted Algernon out of his cage and set him on the dresser for a better look. Then she sat down again beside Emma on the bed to watch the mouse stand up straight against the vase, the little whiskers sniff-sniffing at the drift of each different smell.

Emma said, "Katria, how would you and Algernon like an after-school job at my flower store?"

Katria lay back on her pillow, Algernon snuggled in the folds of her bathrobe, and began to read the Algernon story to Algernon.

CHAPTER NINE

Out the front door and turn right, one block over, right again, and there's the flower shop, open at nine, closed at the other nine. Katria's job, four to six, was filling orders and answering the phone. Then, following straight-ahead streets walking this direction, then turn left and left again, and there's the bakery to pick up her special order of donuts made with whole wheat flour fortified with multiple vitamins with real fruit in the middle and ground carrot sprinkles on top.

Then back home for only a minute before out the door and turn left and left and straight ahead to follow the crooked cemetery lanes past fourteen tombstones and turn right and then left ending at Mary McCraney's to sit in the grass and the weeds like Crazy Person talking to Dead Person. Putting it like that sounded so stupid that as Katria was getting up to leave, never to return, glancing back one last time, she noticed something different about the grass and the weeds on the grave next door to Mary's, like they'd been rearranged. A bushy thing that had been at the top of the grave, covering the small stone marker that was set into the earth, was now closer to the middle, and that spot where the grass had been brown was now green.

Well, so what.

But at the gate of the cemetery, she stopped. She had a funny feeling about this. Someone was looking after this grave but at the same time keeping it hidden. She went back and poked around with her foot. The dirt was slightly lower in a rectangle about three feet wide and six feet long. Maybe there was a hole in the coffin and the person buried there had been fat but now was getting thin, so the dirt was filtering into the coffin and the grave was sinking.

Crouching down in the grass she saw it. There it was. She couldn't believe it, all this time she'd spent wandering and looking and swatting at bugs flying around the tombstones, how could she have missed it? Right there in front of her, a small stone marker with the name etched into it in plain lettering: Sarah Boscov. She couldn't believe it. All those weeks spent poking around in the grass, sometimes after a rain almost stepping on a dew worm, the fat kind, big as snakes, there in that exact spot, she had never noticed, right beside Mary McCraney, like they were neighbours.

...

In her bedroom, under her midnight covers, Katria began to feel like she was surrounded by weird lights and spooky blue haloes floating her to the cemetery to hang out with the undead spirit of her mother and Mary McCraney. Katria thought that maybe all this time hanging out in the graveyard had made her psychic, like those ghost hunters who had taken pictures using infrared cameras of the spirits floating around in that cemetery in New Orleans. They couldn't bury the dead people because of the high sea levels, so the spirits didn't disconnect themselves from the body. They hung out, sort of. So Katria knew that because she had been hanging out, sitting quietly in the grass beside Mary McCraney next to her mother's grave like she was sitting quietly in the church, her mother had been hanging out too, trying to make a connection.

Now Katria knew that, although most dead people had relatives who visited and brought flowers, no one came to visit and bring flowers to her mother. Otherwise, Katria would have seen them. So, the obvious conclusion was that Comrade Ivan had not told the friends and the relatives that Sarah was dead.

Then one late evening, a couple of days before Renata's birthday, just as dark was coming, she saw with her own eyes looking into her bedroom mirror a shadow mother darkening her doorway and entering her room, not walking, but floating, as if Moms's graveyard spirit had followed Katria home. Then in the mirror she saw how thin her mother had become. Hands that used to be chubby had become boney; legs that used to be stove pipes were now sticks.

At first Katria refused to believe what she was seeing. She was hallucinating, probably from listening to the day and night yowling of the cats in the backyard down the street. Or the day and night crying of the baby next door. Then, she didn't know why, maybe it was the power of suggestion from spending so much time thinking graveyard thoughts, she heard her mother say it, almost out loud: You and I, Katria, we are still Tim Hortons double-doubles. But now I'm thin, so you should be thin.

In the repetition of double-double Katria heard the gobble-gobble of the maggots that had all this time been in her mother's coffin busily taking away the fat and bringing in the thin. Katria thought if she caught some of these maggots, each one a cell of her mother, and, like in grade ten biology, kept them in beakers in her bedroom and fed them good food, not that rhubarb crap, they would squirm through the dirt back into her mother's coffin, morph from decayed dead into undecayed undead and from there spread wings to fly with the spirits of the walking dead. Then she could teach them to speak English so they could ask her mother all those questions. They could carry the answers like homing pigeons delivering messages back and forth from the dead to the living, cemetery to bedroom, so Katria wouldn't need to go out the door and turn left and left and straight ahead to follow the crooked cemetery lanes past fourteen tombstones and turn right and then left ending at Mary McCraney to sit in the grass and the weeds like Crazy Person talking to Dead Person.

Then she thought, This is all stupid, I'm never going near this cemetery again. The things that go on in a person's mind, how did this even get started?

CHAPTER TEN

Renata had stopped by Ivan's house to get her mail. Katria wasn't home from school yet so Renata went upstairs to see Algernon. He was curled up in his little basket, stiff as a board. She sat on the bed and considered how she'd break the news to Katria. Maybe he had a tumor or diabetes or something. Maybe he had just died of old age. Renata phoned Emma in the flower shop.

Renata imagined Emma standing at the counter at the back where she did her preps, one hand holding the phone, the other hand fidgeting with the telephone wire, wondering what to do.

Finally, Emma said, "Katria starts work here at four. What should I say?"

"Tell her he died of old age?"

"No, that won't work. Katria will know how he died. She sits Algernon beside her on her desk, his little ears twitching, tilting into every little sound as she searches the web for information on mice. If he was sick, she'd know. If he was old, she'd know. And Renata, if he's been poisoned, she'll know. Even if she doesn't know, she'll blame Ivan for doing it and Katria will get even. I'm beginning to see she has her mother's looks but her father's personality. Relentless. She's got that Tim Hortons article hidden under her mattress. She's got copies of all those zombie movies. They're all about getting plugged into the dead, undead, walking dead, risen dead, whatever kind of dead. I found more pictures of Sarah hidden away in Katria's dresser. When I look at those pictures of Sarah, I see Katria. It's really creepy. Scary, in fact. Ivan told her if she didn't start eating proper food, the mouse would die. And now the mouse has died she'll blame him, and she'll poison him. You heard her say it."

"Yeah, well, she didn't mean it. Just teenage drama."

"Teenage drama? It's way beyond that. This is *Revenge of the Undead*."

CHAPTER ELEVEN

Katria was thinking: Comrade Ivan called his business Guaranteed Gone, but if he guaranteed gone'd all the rats, eventually he'd run out of rats. So, what he probably did was seal up all exit points but one and lay out enough warfarin to drive them outside, but not enough to kill them. Two days later he'd seal the last exit. The only guarantee was he'd receive another call from an address down the street to exterminate the rats he'd just got paid to exterminate. This was like having your donut and eating it too. So, when Katria found the articles Emma had printed, Katria watched the Dr. Chan video. But, she thought, for Comrade Ivan to use ten-eighty on rats would make no sense; but to use ten-eighty on Moms would make lots of sense.

Katria knew that the torn-down Grocery Terminal building next door to the cemetery must have been full of rats, for now they scrambled and scurried between the tombstones and chewed on the wreaths and flowers and ate anything they could find. Katria had spent so much time sitting at Dead Mary's grave talking with her mother that the cemetery rats were coming right up to her, sniff-sniffing for a bite of her pretzels.

She figured, if they could chew through the brick walls and into the concrete foundation to get into the Grocery Terminal, they could burrow through the dirt and into graves and chew through the wood and into the coffins to chew on the bones of the dead people. She knew from listening to Comrade Ivan that each generation of rats was smarter than the one before. They could live in any kind of condition and could raise four litters a year no matter where they were and, according to the Comrade, rubbing his hands together at the thought, compared to all the planetary disasters that were coming, the rat plague would be the worst.

Katria sat in the grass next to Dead Mary. Katria imagined the rats scrambling from coffin to coffin picking up bones as they followed a network of tunnels as big as furnace ducts, like underground cemetery lanes curving the same dusty roads as the ones above, each one ending at a screw-nailed wooden coffin held together by the press of the dirt until, so full of chewed-out holes, it collapsed in splinters. She imagined the rats gathering up the bones, scampering through the groundwater sewer pipes which ran in a vertical line beyond the cemetery gate to the main sewer under the street, climbing by claw-holds on seams in the pipes and up through the manholes onto the pavement, scratching along the slippery asphalt of Ivan's freshly hosed driveway and slipping through that one hole he hadn't yet found to patch, tracking through wall cavities to the kitchen for a quick snack before climbing the stairs, the scrape of their claws scuttling along the upper hall and into his bedroom to tuck Moms's bones under the covers of Ivan's empty bed. On his bedside table they would leave a note: This is for not killing my sixteen wives and all my sisters and our three hundred children and grandchildren and oh yes, my favourite, Uncle Clifford.

The thought of what a surprise waited for Comrade Ivan when he came up the stairs, into his bedroom bed where, oh my gosh, as he turned back the covers to lie himself down to sleep, there her bones lay, laid out so much like Sarah that he'd say, "Sarah? Is that you? Is that what you look like now that you've laid off the donuts and lost all that weight?"

But Katria didn't want the rats to put her mother's bones back in Ivan's bed. No way. Even if they were nice rats. Which they were.

They would swarm up in the cemetery grass and pile out in troupes among the tombstones, squeaking and chittering in a chorus of excited voices, so happy they were at the thought of returning her mother's bones to the bed she had come from and where she belonged. Yes, I know, and thank you, Mr. Rat, but you're returning the victim to her killer.

CHAPTER TWELVE

She took the bus to the Weiner Packing Plant, one of the buildings that hadn't been torn down. She got off the bus and waited at the stop until dark. She walked past the Weiner plant one time on the opposite side of the street. Except for the occasional passing car, the street was deserted, although the lights were on in all the buildings on both sides, even though it was past eight o'clock. They just left them on all night, she guessed. She noticed that, though the windows across the front of the Weiner Plant were lit up, all the ones along the lane which led to the back were dark. She followed the lane and circled around to try to get in through a rear window. She took four quick steps across the back of the building and slipped along the side to the first basement window. It was shut tight, as was the second, but the third was loose enough that she could slide it upwards — but not enough to allow her to climb through. She jiggled it several times, trying to force it, but it would not budge. She returned to the first one, this time bending close, trying to see if it was latched on the inside. She tried the second, but again no luck. Finally, just as she was about to give up, the third window gave way to her jiggling and broke free. But she didn't lower herself feet first into the opening. She leaned forward and listened. Convinced the building was deserted, she eased herself in.

She hurried across the basement to the steps leading to the main floor. She opened the door and crept along the hallway to the lab door. Inside were lines of cages of white mice and rats, and along one wall jars and packages, all labeled. She scooped three tablespoons from a jar of ten-eighty into a ziplock. She unlatched all the mouse cages before she left.

Not until she stopped to wait for a red traffic light did she relax. She arrived home a little before nine. She went into the kitchen, opened the refrigerator, and made a chicken sandwich with a little mayonnaise and pepper. Once she had finished the sandwich, she rummaged around in the refrigerator until she found an apple, which she ate sitting at the dining room table.

CHAPTER THIRTEEN

Mrs. Rawlins was back for a touch up. "My neighbour asked who did my hair, so I said, 'Renata at The Cutting Corner.' So she said, 'Does she do men's haircuts,' so I said, 'Don't send your husband there. When he sees Renata, he'll get himself so jacked he'll end up pitching his tent.'"

Mrs. Rawlins gave Renata a once-over in the mirror. "My husband is old and fat and slow but he can still get it up, which is what he'd be doing under this cover."

Renata was paying no attention to Mrs. Rawlins's ramblings. In the last week, she had developed carpal tunnel syndrome. He had given her enough pain pills to finish off her booked appointments and said, "Give your hands a few days' rest and book yourself into physiotherapy."

Carpal tunnel syndrome, like arthritis, was the scourge of the hairdresser. But the pill she had taken a half-hour earlier was kicking in and she was feeling dreamy as she worked with the hair, pleased with the way the perm was growing out. Mrs. Rawlins was not frowning the way she had at the first appointment, not squinting into the mirror, watching Renata work. Now she was relaxed. Mrs. Rawlins would be a steady client and would recommend Renata to her friends. Build customers one at a time.

"How long should this perm last?"

"It depends on how fast your hair grows. A customer phoned to complain that her blonde highlights went dark. So I looked up in my system and it said I did the highlights four months ago. So I told her I did it four months ago. So the customer says, 'Yeah so?' So I said, 'Yeah so, hair does what it does and what it does is grow.'"

"It does what it does. My neighbour has a bird feeder. She asked me what the best way to kill a cat is. The goddamn cat hides in the bushes and kills the birds. It killed a whole nest of cardinals. So now she wants to poison the cat. So I said, 'Why not hire that dog poisoner? Then you don't have to kill the cat yourself.'"

"Well," said Renata, "I think the reason people don't do it themselves is that they don't want to hurt the animal. They just want the problem corrected. I know how I'd feel if I found a nest of dead baby birds and the cat sitting there with a mouthful of feathers pretending it didn't have anything to do with it. People should keep their cats indoors."

"Then she found a nest of dead baby rabbits. Same cat. She said, 'I'm going to put out a dish of milk, here kitty-kitty, and when it comes, I'm going to hit it with a hammer.'"

Renata said, "That's what I mean. The animal's behaviour forces the person to fix the problem. It's the same with dogs. I just moved into a small six-plex. The dog next door barks all day and night. So I'm looking for a new apartment. But on the news it said there's a zero vacancy rate, so I'll probably never find one."

All this talk about the dog poisoner had Renata wondering: Ivan needed money to promote his books; he'd loaned Emma money he didn't have. Each time Renata thought about it, she wondered. Ivan? Maybe.

Mrs. Rawlins rambled on; Renata drifted. Listening was part of her job and, although Mrs. Rawlins was a crackpot, she was a likable crackpot, so Renata continued to drift. Until Mrs. Rawlins commented, "It said on the news the dog poisoner drives a white van."

Renata's mirrors didn't shatter but that's what it felt like. She managed, "No kidding."

"The kid reading the news wears a dark-blue suit with a light-blue shirt and dark-blue tie. He looks like a college kid at a wedding. He said the dog poisoner is a professional. He's using ten-eighty, an untraceable poison in a hamburger bait pack wrapped in butcher paper and smeared with tobacco so the raccoons and skunks don't get into it."

Renata needed to change the subject, maybe by shoving a towel in this woman's mouth. She said, "Tomorrow is my twenty-third birthday. My older half-sister and me, we're going to hit the bars."

"Hit the bars! That's dangerous for a girl as pretty as you."

"Yeah, I guess." Renata sighed. "Men. Yeah. The one thing that all men at singles bars have in common is they're all married."

"I wish my husband would go to a singles bar so I could get rid of him."

"Yeah, totally. I've never met a man I didn't want to get rid of."

Aunt Gizla phoned as Mrs. Rawlins was leaving. "Hello Dearie, I have your birthday present ready for you to pick up."

Renata knew what it would be: twenty dollars cash, minus the price of the card, which was usually two-fifty unless she'd bought it at the dollar store.

Renata tidied away her equipment and locked up. The subway was only half a block away, and her aunt's apartment two stops north, on Davisville. As usual, Rolfie got busy in her crotch the moment she walked in the door. As usual, she heard in her mind those long-ago words: Renata. Go into the storage room so Rolfie can't do that. As usual, Aunt Gizla was dressed in a pale-blue blouse and dark-blue slacks, like the boy on the news. As usual, the apartment was neat and tidy, just like Ivan's house.

Aunt Gizla's mind had been programmed like a Russian surveillance computer to sound a warning in her brain whenever anything in her apartment, like a knick-knack or a magazine, was shifted off-grid, so the game for Renata when she was little was to move one item slightly to one side, a napkin in its holder, for example, and sit back and wait for Aunt Gizla's electronics to kick in.

While Aunt Gizla was in her bedroom getting the birthday present, Renata noticed the goldfish, Dr. Goldstein, was dead-centre on the storage room windowsill; she moved the fishbowl two inches to the left. Aunt Gizla returned with the envelope, the toonie and two quarters sliding around inside along with the ten and the five. Then, like a *beep-beep* on a tiny television in Gizla's detail-driven brain, her head swiveled side to side, located the item, and dispatched her body to return Dr. Goldstein to the correct spot.

"Can we drink a vodka toast for my birthday, Aunt Gizla?" Renata didn't want to drink a toast with her aunt, but she did want a drink.

"Of course, that is tradition."

"I'll fix it for you."

Renata made the double shots of vodka with dill pickles, a tradition Grandpa Boris Boscov had brought back from the front. Now, this frontline tradition for Renata was down the hatch, eat the pickle, take the card with seventeen-fifty, and leave to buy two bottles of birthday vodka.

Renata asked Aunt Gizla the question. "Are you still following Ivan's diet?"

"Of course. Good healthy food."

"How do you feel?"

"I feel fine. If Sarah had followed his diet, she wouldn't have been so fat. Ivan was so embarrassed with her, how fat she got. He is a proud man. *Toronto Life* ran an article on him working at home in his kitchen experimenting with the healing powers of rhubarb, losing weight by cleansing the body with Dr. Boscov's ten-speed diet. They had him on the front cover riding a ten-speed. The next day the *Sun* printed that photo of Sarah looking like she weighed five-hundred pounds, just when he was getting his health food business started. He was working on a deal for rhubarb ketchup and rhubarb salad dressing with his picture on the bottle, riding a ten-speed."

"He doesn't even have a ten-speed. He's a complete quack. Katria thinks he poisoned Sarah because she ruined his phoney business."

"Katria needs a good swat on the backside."

Renata paused before asking the other question that had been bugging her since her conversations with Mrs. Rawlins. "Have you heard about the dog poisoner?"

"Of course."

"Remember that little brown dog down the street died? It was cute as a button dressed up in a red outfit for its daily walk. The old lady was British. She talked like the queen. She called the dog Knottingley. I think if Ivan killed little dogs like that, I'd kill him myself."

Aunt Gizla fanned the air, a habit learned from Nana, batting anything you said back at you. "In the war they fed little dogs like that to the children."

Renata left and walked to the subway. She had no appointments until two. Ivan would be home at noon, making his lunch, his white van parked in the drive, the spare keys in a magnetic clip hidden in the rear bumper. He was a lock nut. Everything needed ten locks so he wouldn't be robbed and because he had all these locks, he needed to have ten spare keys, and in case he was ever robbed of the spare keys, he had more spare keys.

Renata used the hidden keys to open the back door of the van. She climbed in. The sides had been paneled with labelled hooks to hang various lights and tools. Behind the driver's seat was a locked cupboard, the key hidden exactly where you might expect, in the glove compartment. There were several packages of warfarin as well as labelled cleaners, scrub brushes, and hand soaps. She recognized the insecticide smell of the soap Ivan washed his hands with fifty times a day. An unlabelled jar that looked like salt was wedged between two boxes of warfarin.

She locked everything up, replaced the keys, and hurried away.

CHAPTER FOURTEEN

Emma noted the exact time of the call from Aunt Gizla's landlord: 3:45 p.m., September 10. When she got there, the landlord explained, "Ivan wasn't answering his phone but I found Renata's number on Gizla's calendar. Renata said to phone you. She sounded kind of out of it."

"It's her birthday. She got an early start on the celebrations, I guess. I'll come over right away."

Emma pulled up at the front of the high-rise on Davisville at four fifteen and parked behind a waiting ambulance and a Humane Society van with a driver inside. He said, "The dog's in the truck."

"So why the ambulance?"

"There were two calls. First, the lady called saying the dog'd been poisoned, and then she called 911 saying *she'd* been poisoned."

"Is she all right?"

He was playing with his cellphone. He didn't look up. He muttered, "Don't think so."

This was Emma's first time at this apartment, but it was about what she expected from Aunt Gizla: flowered chesterfield and matching flowered chair; dark oak end tables and matching dark oak coffee table with dark-brown coffee-table book placed squarely in its centre.

The paramedics, one male and one female, were packing up to leave. Aunt Gizla was stretched out on her back on the floor of a walk-in closet, as though she had lain down to take a nap. As Emma drew closer, she thought she could smell bug-killer.

A voice behind her said, "The skin colour indicates cardiac arrest."

The tag on her paramedic's uniform said "Ashley."

Emma stepped back. "She's dead?"

"Afraid so."

"Has Ivan been here? Her brother Ivan?"

"Don't think so."

Emma sniffed at the smell. "The Humane Society driver mentioned poison."

"If there was enough poison to kill her, she'd have been vomiting, you know, convulsions, delusional. There's no sign of that — I think ventricular arrhythmia. We're waiting for another call."

"So why would she say she was poisoned?"

Unlike the Humane Society character, Ashley showed some sympathy. "The probable explanation? Often the early symptoms of heart failure are upset stomach and nausea. So, she found the dog dead, had a heart attack, thought they were both poisoned, and called 911."

Emma stared down at the body with a mixture of revulsion and curiosity. She backed away two steps but then came up for a closer look. "Is there something not right about this? The way she's lying stiff and straight flat on her back in the storage room as though she'd been placed there ... And I'm still smelling insecticide."

"It smells to me like toilet-bowl cleaner."

Emma checked the toilet. No signs of vomit, but judging from the cleanliness of the apartment, if she'd been sick, she'd have cleaned up after herself before she lay down to die. Not unusual for a Boscov neat freak, her last ounce of energy spent leaving everything tidy, in this case the toilet especially.

Emma wandered into the living room. Across from the television sat a recliner chair and on a little table next to it sat two bundles of wool, one blue and one gray, and two knitting needles. Emma could not recognize what was being knit, for the ball of wool had been unravelled and the needles had been bent, as though the knitter had grown impatient and tried to destroy her work. Emma's mother liked to knit, late at night, unable to sleep, sitting in her recliner, but Emma had never seen her destroy her knitting.

Aunt Gizla's purse, which was sitting on the dining room table, contained a Russian birth certificate, two credit cards, and fifty-five dollars in cash. Emma checked the kitchen cupboards, but there was no sign of anything out of the ordinary. The kitchen was tidy, no unwashed dishes except for a glass which seemed to have been rinsed before it was placed upside down in the sink. Emma remembered the Boscov obsession. Each time she had a glass of something, rinse it out, then upside down in the sink.

She sat at the kitchen table. From this vantage point, she could see the attendant, Ashley, now leaning against the wall, talking on her cell. She was young, mid-twenties, her hair pulled back in a ponytail. No makeup. Capable-looking.

When Ashley finished on the phone, Emma asked, "What should I be doing?"

"Waiting for the coroner."

"I have a question. My fourteen-year-old sister has been on a junk food, nothing-but-donuts diet. And now all of a sudden on an eat-nothing diet. She won't go to the doctor. If I call an ambulance, will they take her to the hospital?"

Ashley sat across from her. "We get junk food calls sometimes. They're from husbands of wives on diet fads, you know, some diet guru will say nothing but fruit or nothing but vegetables, so these people are starving. There's the tapeworm diet, the baby food diet, the five-bite diet. You don't consume it; it consumes you."

"Like alcohol."

"The same. A silent battle in your head that might last an entire day: whether or not to have one slice of bread. Your body is crying out for food like it cries out for water. Food, food everywhere but not a bite to eat. But not all fad diets are harmful. I mean, what the heck, you could probably live on Big Macs for a long time without any consequences."

"Have you ever heard of the rhubarb diet?"

Ashley shook her head. "That's a new one." She tapped her cellphone and gave it a quick glance, then laid it on the table.

Emma asked. "So can I call an ambulance on her?"

"Sure. They'll do her vitals, but even if they're low, they can't force her to do anything she doesn't want to do. Not unless she's collapsed and gone into a coma, or her vitals are so low she's close to death."

"She's killing herself with junk food and no one can do anything about it?"

"You're only the sister so the father or mother would be the one to get her committed. Although, in parasuicide, the aim is not death. It's a disguised call for help."

Ashley sounded as though she actually cared in a job that needed a tough exterior. "I guess you've seen it all."

Ashley shrugged. "It's called being a paramedic."

"Why did you get into this line of work?"

She thought a minute. "Because of my mom and dad probably."

"Following in their footsteps?"

"Not exactly ... sort of. I'd come home from school and find my mom overdosed on the living room couch so I'd phone the ambulance and take a book out on the front step and wait for them to come. I knew she was never in any real danger. And my dad was an alcoholic. Sometimes I'd wake up in the night and come downstairs and find him passed out on the floor or the front lawn or the sidewalk. So I'd phone the ambulance. They came to my house so often I got to know all the paramedics. 'Hi Ashley,' they'd say. Sometimes I'd ask them to help me with my homework."

"How old were you?"

"Nine, ten, eleven ... It went on forever."

"And you didn't turn out screwed up?"

"Screwed up, no. Street smart, yes. *Detached* might be a better word. It was self-preservation. Lots of time as I sat on the porch, I thought, Why do I bother to call the ambulance? Why not let them poison themselves? Get it over with. Maybe go in there and help them along a little bit. But then I'd think, I've got a roof over my head, there's food in the fridge. My father was a cook in a pub, an alcoholic, yes, but a functional alcoholic, not unusual in the pub business."

"So you turned out okay."

"Yes, because of one of the paramedics in particular. She was young, about the age I am now. She'd come over on her day off and we'd hang out. So it was just natural for me to go into the line of work I was most familiar with."

Ashley's face was thoughtful; it showed no anger and no hostility. "Don't you carry any ... you know, baggage?"

"None, except for every life I've seen lost, I think of my parents throwing their lives away. But it is what it is. Why bother worrying about how it should be? Maybe how it is is how it should be. They both wasted their lives and died early. It is what it is. That's my philosophy. I don't let it bother me."

"Any chance you could talk with my sister? I think she needs to hear your story. She needs to hear your attitude."

"I'm not allowed. Not unless, of course, you call 911 and say she's in a coma and I happen to take the call. Which is unlikely."

Ashley's cellphone rang. "Good luck with your sister."

When Emma wandered into the bedroom, she noticed a goldfish bowl sitting on the windowsill. She remembered that both Aunt Gizla and Nana always had a goldfish that they called Dr. Goldstein. Next to Dr. Goldstein sat an open container of fish food. Specks of it floated in the water above the goldfish. Emma was certain that Aunt Gizla would have put the top back on the container. So, either Aunt Gizla had been feeding the goldfish right before she died and had not been able to put the top back on, or someone else had fed the goldfish immediately after Aunt Gizla died and not bothered about it.

Emma took a picture of the knitting and the fish food with her cellphone. Then, back in the kitchen, she took pictures of the food in the refrigerator, which was well stocked with Ivan's rhubarb concoctions plus yogurt, fruit, juice, normal stuff. The leftover rhubarb concoctions were sealed in containers. She opened the crisper: fresh lettuce, green beans, apples, and several garlic cloves. She checked the codes on the milk and the cheese. She smelled everything that was wrapped in saran. There was no evidence of food gone bad in containers. She took a picture of Ivan's diet books, which were sitting on the kitchen table. She took pictures of the open cupboards: rolled oats, unsalted nuts, wheat germ, the healthy lifestyle of someone who apparently had fed the goldfish without resealing the top, unravelled her knitting, bent her knitting needles, and lay down on the storage room floor and died.

Emma's childhood image of Aunt Gizla was of her sitting at the kitchen table, her back straight as she ate her yogurt with nuts and berries. Then she'd get up immediately to wash the dishes and tidy everything away, and scrub and clean and disinfect, then lie down for her nap on her bed.

Emma went back to the storage room. She got down on her hands and knees. Her top-to-bottom sniff of Aunt Gizla ended at the smell she had noticed earlier: freshly painted black nail-polished toes, so fresh the lacquer hadn't hardened.

Emma returned to the kitchen where she noticed stuck by a magnet to the refrigerator door a white business card: Ivan Boscov, Guaranteed Gone Rodent Removal. A second card was for The Cutting Corner: Renata Boscov. On the back was written "Renata's B'day Sept 10," which was today. In two hours, Renata would be waiting for her at her favourite bar, The Header.

Emma left the apartment unlocked for the coroner and started down the hall toward the elevator.

Emma fought the traffic to a pet store on Avenue Road. The clerk showed her three kinds of fish food. She bought one of them and drove to her store. When she noticed the sign on the window was not flipped from closed to open, she remembered that Katria had said she was staying late at school.

Emma poured water into a Styrofoam cup, added a pinch of fish food, and sat down to time how long it took to sink to the bottom. Approximately thirty minutes. So Gizla Boscov had fed the goldfish, phoned 911 twice, cleaned up her sick mess, painted her nails biker-chick black, lay down on the floor in the storage room, and died. Then the ambulance arrived, then Emma arrived. All in the space of thirty minutes.

Didn't add up.

CHAPTER FIFTEEN

Emma phoned Renata. She sounded tipsy. "Cancel The Header? Are you kidding? That's all the more reason to celebrate."

Emma arrived first and waited at the front entrance of the bar. Ten minutes later, Renata appeared, looking beautiful in her red A-line dress with matching six-inch spikes.

They took a seat in a booth near the back. Renata said, "He's mad that neither me nor Katria want anything to do with Aunt Gizla's funeral arrangements. He says if we don't come to the funeral and to the reception and whatever else he's got planned he'll disown us both. So I said, 'Can't wait. Where do I sign.'"

Emma asked the question that was troubling her. "Did Aunt Gizla ever paint her toenails black?"

"Aunt Gizla? No way."

"Hmm. I noticed Aunt Gizla is following Ivan's diet."

"She was. I know. Why do you bring it up? What are you thinking?" Renata gave Emma a stern don't-think-it look. "No way. Ivan wouldn't poison his Comrade Sister."

"Not intentionally, but the other day I saw a programme on a plant-based poison called ten-eighty. First Sarah, now Aunt Gizla."

"No way, Emma."

Emma dropped it. She glanced around, then back to Renata. "Is this where you meet Mr. Right? If so, the Mr. Rights will be crumpling to their knees over you. You look great."

Renata ordered straight vodka and a pickle. "This is the only bar that serves them this way. One shot down the hatch and then a bite of pickle. The brine in the pickle mellows out the vodka. No hangover."

The drinks arrived. They clinked glasses. Emma said, "The reason I left, never to return, was that I didn't want to be a Russian Boscov. And here I am drinking it like a Russian Boscov. It feels like I'm renewing my citizenship."

"It feels like I'm celebrating a birthday. Here's to me!"

Renata downed her drink. Emma took a sip. She said, "Don't look now but that guy at the end of the bar has his eye on you. He looks like a drug dealer."

Renata snuck a look at a man with sunglasses perched on a shaved head, a fashionable two-days' growth of stubble, a leather jacket with lots of zippered pockets, and fashionably ripped and tight jeans over fashionable cowboy boots. He was showing the bartender pictures on his cellphone but his eyes were on Renata.

Renata said, "One time I was in here and I did meet a guy who looked like Mr. Right. We had a few drinks, me a few too many, and I was feeling sick, so I went into the lady's room. After a few minutes, he came in and told the women standing around putting on their makeup that he was a doctor and wanted to make sure I was all right. He wanted to come into the cubicle with me."

"And did he?"

"Are you kidding? I was sick."

"The dealer has his eye on you."

When Renata glanced over again, he got up, hiked up his jeans, straightened his untucked shirt, and turned up the collar of his leather jacket. Drink in hand, he approached.

"Can I buy you a drink?" he said to Renata.

"My sister thinks you look like a drug dealer."

"I work undercover."

"Show me your badge."

He sat beside her. "It's my night off. Can I buy you a drink?"

"I'm taking painkillers so I have to take it easy. But okay, just one."

CHAPTER SIXTEEN

Renata awoke flat on her back in a hospital bed, knee throbbing, ankle aching. A doctor came in. "Ah, good. You're awake. You've had a bit of a bad fall, Renata. I'm Dr. McLeod. Do you remember how it happened?"

"I fell off the subway platform."

Dr. McLeod pulled back the sheets to examine her ankle. "How did you fall off the subway platform?"

Renata tried to remember. "I was wearing new heels so I was kind of wobbly. And I was drunk. Too much vodka. I'm Russian."

"Boscov. Yes. But you don't have an accent."

"I was born here."

Dr. McLeod ran his hand from the ankle to the knee and back again, checking for whatever. She liked the feel of his hand.

"It says here in the report that you jumped, Renata."

"Well, I didn't."

"And you won't do it again?"

Renata sat up. "I have to go to work. What time is it?"

"Today is Sunday. You work Sunday?"

"No."

Dr. McLeod pulled over the chrome-legged chair from the end of the bed. "I'm an orthopedic surgeon. Dr. Enright called me in."

Dr. McLeod examined her leg and her foot.

He was middle-aged, Renata noted, with longish hair, and kind of cute; he was probably older than he looked. Now that she was sitting up, the painkillers the nurse had given her seemed to be kicking in a little stronger. She didn't mind him picking up her foot.

"These are good painkillers," she said. Too good, she thought, added to the vodka she had been drinking the night before. There might have been a shooter or two in there, plus the painkillers for her hands … She was fried.

"It's a bad sprain, but nothing is broken. I'm going to write you a prescription for a week of painkillers and suggest you limit your walking for a few days. Soft tissue damage is more painful than a fracture, but it heals a lot quicker."

Renata examined her leg. "What about my knee?"

"Scraped it when you jumped, I guess."

"I didn't jump."

Dr. McLeod got up and carried the chair to the opposite wall. Comrade Ivan would say, Renata, that chair was at the end of the bed so that's where it belongs since that's where it was when the doctor dragged it over to the bedside.

The doctor left. A nurse came in with a tray and a glass of water. She handed Renata a yellow pill.

"To help with the pain," she said.

Renata thought, If I'm here for the rest of the day, I might as well enjoy it. She swallowed the pill, lay back in the bed and tried to remember what happened the night before. Emma had left her in The Header with the drug dealer guy and gone home. She remembered that much but not much else as she drifted off to sleep.

...

When Renata woke up, her head a little clearer, she remembered the dealer's name was Vance and he was not undercover. But after he had bought her all those vodkas, he suggested, insisted more like it, she go home with him. This she didn't want to do. So, while he was in the washroom, she went out to the street. There were no cabs but the subway entrance was right there.

"Renata Boscov? I'm Dr. Enright."

Like the last doctor, he pulled up the chair to sit next to her.

"I'm to give you a psychiatric assessment."

"Why?"

"Yesterday your aunt died quite suddenly, and then a few hours later you jumped off a subway platform."

"I didn't jump."

"Well according to the police report, you did." He adjusted his suit jacket and leaned forward and gave her a stern look. "I do mental health assessments two or three times a week for the police and the courts."

He was scowling at the leg which she had left uncovered. He didn't pick it up or reach out and run his hand up and down like the last doctor, although she wished he would. He was even cuter than the other one and much younger.

"Do you understand what I just said, Renata?"

"You do assessments."

He said, "A rubber band refuses to give more than two or three inches. When you let go, it contracts back to its original size. Or like a desk lamp that folds back into itself. Pull at it again and again, let it go and watch it fold back into the way it was. Sometimes we can open a patient up almost straight but as soon as they're released, they will fold back the way they were. That's why we keep them here for as long as we can, so they don't fold back into themselves when we let them go."

"Elastic bands? Desk lights? "What are you talking about?"

"After I do the assessment you'll be turned over to one of the staff doctors. After you've been with us a while, depending on the police assessment, you can get a weekend pass. To see how you make out."

"A weekend pass for a sprained ankle?"

"Well, not yet. After you've been with us awhile."

"Then I get the weekend pass? To where?"

She blinked, double-blinked, trying to get him out of split-ends double focus so that she could understand what he was talking about.

She tried to triple-blink the room into single focus. Across from her, the wall was bare white. There was no furniture except for the one chair and her bed. There was one window covered with heavy fencing wire.

She turned her attention to the doctor, who was explaining something about how weekend passes aren't given, they're earned.

"Earned? What do I have to do?" Now she began to wonder if she was having an erotic dream. Invite the cute doctor into her bed and she'd get a free weekend pass.

"You have to try your best and cooperate with the staff."

"How many staff are there?"

"On this ward, five nurses on the day shift and three on the night shift."

"Male nurses, you mean?"

"Female nurses. Trained psychiatric nurses."

"Psychiatric? What kind of hospital is this?"

"This is the Monroe Institute. You were admitted last night. Don't you remember?"

"Of course I don't remember, I was reeling drunk."

"Well ... here you are."

"For a sprained ankle?"

"You jumped off the subway platform."

"Who told you that? I fell."

"Yes, I know. You fell."

The doctor got up and left. He didn't return the chair to the foot of the bed and Renata didn't feel like getting up to do it, no matter what Comrade Ivan had to say about it. She lay back on the bed and drifted with the meds. They were better than vodka, dreamier. That Dr. Enright, he was a dream. I should get up and brush my hair. All these cute doctors, horny nurses, weekend passes ... I'm going to like it here.

After a while, Dr. Enright came back with what must have been the head nurse and they talked about Renata's condition, but she could not follow what they were saying. An hour earlier, her mind had been working fine. Well, a bit dreamy. But now she could not understand anything. Her mind was caught in riddles. She tried to put together what had happened but she was confused about different times and different events and she didn't know if she was at Headers two days ago or yesterday and didn't know when she fell off the subway platform or how long she'd been in the hospital. Like a riddle: did she do this on that day or that on this day and what happened after what, and why? Her tongue was too thick to talk and her thoughts, any that she could put together, were not at all like thoughts, merely something vaguely smothered inside whispering, "Holy gosh! They think I jumped off the subway platform."

Another nurse arrived. Miss Jordan, she said her name was. Tall and thin with stringy grey hair. She needs a hair wash, thought Renata. Holy gosh. Another painkiller. And soon and soon there would be Miss Jordan with another painkiller. I'm liking this place just fine. I don't care one bit that I'm in the mental hospital, my scissors retired, my chairs empty, and here I am not caring about anything but the bed under my back and my brain whirling riddles in my mind but holy gosh they think I jumped off the subway platform! Well, for that, I get a free weekend pass with that cute doctor. And sleep with the nurses. She wasn't too sure about the nurses. She'd never tried that.

Miss Jordan again: "The doctor says you should try and walk a bit, Renata."

"I think the doctor needs to think again."

"Just a little exercise. Move around a little."

Renata tried to blink the nurse out of double focus. Either there were two Renatas or two nurses. This wasn't Miss Jordan. This one was skinny as a pole with so much lipstick her mouth looked like red plastic. Renata closed her eyes. If she was too stoned to get out of bed, she was too stoned to think about lipstick.

"That was yesterday," said the nurse in answer to something Renata had said; she had no idea what. "Now you start to walk on it."

"I know. But these painkillers, they make me stupid."

"Your body is adjusting. You'll soon be feeling normal. Get out of bed. We'll walk down the hall to the lounge."

Renata hoisted herself out of bed. Steadying herself with her right fist against the wall, she began the walk down the hall to the lounge. But she could not keep track of where she was, where the floor was, where the nurse was. Renata tried to make her way to the chair the nurse was pointing at but she seemed unable to judge space and distance. She seemed unable to tell where her sprained foot was in relationship to the floor, making it impossible to place it in front of the other.

Renata's eyes shifted out of focus again as the walls tilted to the right and the chairs in the lounge slid from their places along the wall.

"Here you go, Renata." Miss Jordan appeared from somewhere and caught one as it slid past. "Sit down here, Renata, next to Elaine."

Renata sat where she was told.

Elaine said, "What's the matter with your eyes?"

Renata could not find an answer.

"Blink," Elaine ordered.

Renata blinked Elaine into a hazy focus. Elaine looked too young and too deranged to be a nurse, although since everything in Renata's mind was jumbled it was hard to tell

Elaine blinked back.

"You have a low blink rate," said Elaine. "That's oxys. Miss Jordan, this little bitch is taking oxys. Miss Jordan? She's on oxys. They slow down your blinks."

Renata leaned back and drifted off and when she woke up her ankle was too swollen to bend. She limped back to her room and sat in the chair at the foot of her bed. After a while a different nurse arrived with two more painkillers.

"I don't want any more pills."

"Doctor's orders. You have to take them."

Renata tried to take the pills. She reached out with her right hand to take one. But she could not get her fingers unclenched. Each finger seemed unaware of the other and each seemed unable to tell how far it was to the pills or where the pills were on the tray or which fingers were supposed to pick them up.

The nurse picked up the pills. Her fingers scooped them up and held them. Her left hand swept through the air and plucked them from the tray. Renata tried to take one but, unable to judge the distance, her fist closed on empty air. The nurse caught her hand and held it.

The nurse returned the pills to her tray. "Have you been taking unprescribed drugs, Renata? I'm calling Heinz for a room search."

Renata tried to explain that she wanted to go home and that these painkillers were too strong and the doctor made a mistake and she shouldn't be here. But abruptly her eyes shifted into the shadows and her brain shut down and her thoughts stopped coming and her words were silenced and she was unable to sort feeling into words, thoughts into sentences. Her head fell back against the chair.

After a while a nurse called Miss Little came with a towel and soap to escort her to her bathroom. Renata expected the nurse would go away and leave her in the washroom in private, but instead she stood in the doorway and, while the water ran into the sink, stared at Renata's reflection in the mirror.

"If you're going to stand there watching me, I'm not washing anything. And you can forget about the free pass stuff. I've changed my mind. I want to go home."

"Not feeling too good, eh? What are you on, Renata, besides those painkillers?"

"My clothes are what I'm on. I'd like my clothes back."

"Clothes are for level one. You're not level one."

"Then put me on level one."

"I don't think you'll be getting privileges for a while, Renata. Especially not if Heinz finds drugs hidden in your room. Wash your face, you look terrible."

Renata was too tired to wash her face.

"Has this got something to do with your Aunt Gizla's death?" asked the nurse.

"Aunt Gizla? She's dead?"

"Are you upset about Aunt Gizla?"

"Since when is Aunt Gizla dead?"

"Since yesterday. Is that why you're upset?'

"I hate Aunt Gizla."

"Hate is a strong word, Renata."

Holy gosh, thought Renata. I forgot she died. Oh my gosh. I better stop saying I hate her. They'll think I killed her. That's why the windows are covered with twelve-gauge wire. Oh my god … And the doctor said something about the police … Oh my gosh.

The nurse helped Renata back to her bed. Through the open doorway and across the lounge she could see Elaine at the elevator, pressing the buttons, first with one finger of one hand and then with the same finger on the other hand. She seemed to be constantly losing count and starting again.

Heinz, a tall, balding man, arrived. He searched her room and discovered in her purse the pills the doctor had given her for carpal tunnel syndrome. He left, taking his prize with him.

CHAPTER SEVENTEEN

Now Renata was in Dr. Enright's office. The clock on the wall said it was two. How it got to be two o'clock she didn't know. But she knew how she got to the doctor's office. Miss Little brought her.

Dr. Enright was saying, "Only level one patients wear their own clothes, Renata, and only after they've been with us a long time and have a positive record."

"What positive record? There's nothing wrong with my record. Give me my clothes. I want to go home."

Dr. Enright opened his laptop. "Nothing wrong with your record? Last night you jumped off a subway platform."

"I must be hallucinating, right? Or dead, right? I fell off the subway platform and got run over by the train and now I'm mashed potatoes, right? Like what do you get after you mash a potato? Mashed potatoes. I'm having one of those after-death experiences? That's what's going on, right? So who are you? God?"

"I'm Dr. Enright. And yes, you're hallucinating that you didn't jump and you didn't sprain your ankle and scrape your knee but no, you are not mashed potatoes. If that's what you feel like, it's because you've been taking oxycodone as well as the painkillers we've been giving you plus you have a hangover from the vodka."

"Vodka? I'm Russian. Emma and I were celebrating. And yes, some kind of painkiller for my carpal tunnel. I think what happened was I mixed the vodka and the painkillers and blacked out and fell off the subway platform and — and I want my clothes back!"

'Why are you so worried about your clothes?"

She got up and opened her hospital-issue robe so he could see her hospital-issue PJs. "Look how they dress me. The top is too tight and the bottom is falling off and the robe doesn't do up right."

Renata noticed Dr. Enright steal a glance at the open robe as he pulled his chair closer to his desk and began to slide his mouse around on his laptop screen. "Any history of mental illness in the family?"

She sat down. "My father. He's crazy."

"In what way, Renata?"

"He poisons anything that crawls, walks, or flies. Maybe he poisoned me. It sure feels like it."

Dr. Enright frowned. He let go of his mouse to make a note on a pad to the right of his desk.

"What I mean, Dr. Enright, is he has an animal control business. Guaranteed Gone. He drives a white van, unmarked so no one knows he's there to poison something. I think he put poison in my vodka."

Dr. Enright slid his mouse in a circle off to one side and clicked.

"I'm just kidding, Doctor, if the checkbox you just clicked was Paranoid or Delusional, uncheck it. Those pain pills made me feel like I'd been poisoned. That's what I meant to say."

Dr. Enright's slid his mouse up and down, back and forth. Bingo.

"Dr. Enright?"

"Yes, Renata?"

"Are you a real doctor? And if you are, don't you have a secretary who can click a mouse on checkboxes? Or are you ordering us a pizza?"

He looked up from his laptop.

Renata continued. "First you have to stop playing with that stupid mouse and fold your hands on your desk. Folding your hands on the desk is a signal that you are more interested in listening to the patient than you are in fondling your mouse. Here is all you need to know.

Write it on your little pad: Number one, Renata fell off the subway platform; number two, Renata wants to go home."

"You're here for an assessment, Renata. You're very lucky to be here at all. Someone noticed you lying on the tracks, someone phoned the suicide hotline, someone phoned 911. Someone on the TTC crew radioed a slowdown for the next train. Any or all of the above saved you from being mashed potatoes. You told the police you were visiting Aunt Gizla, so they dispatched a unit to her address and found her suspiciously dead."

When Renata had arrived at Dr. Enright's door, her thoughts had been cloudy. Suddenly they became clear. "Oh my god. Wow. Yeah. I see what you mean. Maybe we should drag that mouse back to the beginning and start again."

Dr. Enright got up and took off his suit jacket and rolled up his sleeves and sat back down. "Back to the assessment. No smartass comments, Renata. Let's get this done."

Renata leaned forward. "Just one thing before we start. Why would I jump off a subway platform, Dr. Enright?"

He shrugged. "Why do people do what they do? Why do people knock a little white ball back and forth across a field? Why do people put boards on their feet and slide down a snow-covered hill and then when they reach bottom go back up to the top and do the same thing? The Myth of Sisyphus. The behaviour makes sense only to the one doing it."

"That's what I mean. Jumping off the subway platform makes no sense to me. Just like you wearing proper clothes and me not wearing proper clothes makes no sense to me. In fact, it pisses me off. But to you, it must make sense because you decided I shouldn't wear proper clothes. So, explain to me: why did you do that?"

Dr. Enright frowned. He tilted his head in a questioning stare. "Why this insistence on wearing street clothes? This is a hospital. In a hospital you wear hospital clothes."

"Why when I was talking about not wearing clothes did syphilis pop into your head?" Renata settled back in her chair. She pulled the hospital bathrobe up to her chin.

"The word was Sisyphus. Back to the question."

"We never left the question. But okay. I guess wearing hospital clothes would make sense if I was planning to stay in the hospital and it would make sense for you to dress me in PJs if you were planning to keep me in the hospital. But not over the winter, I'd need a hospital coat for catching the bus for my weekend pass. But it's not winter and I'm not planning to stay."

Dr. Enright almost smiled. "That's for me to decide, Renata, depending on how this appointment goes." He swung his mouse to some target on his screen. "Let's get back to the assessment. Tell me about Aunt Gizla."

Renata sighed. She closed her eyes. "In my line of work, finding patience is sometimes a struggle. So what I do is I close my eyes and count to ten. Okay. Done. Okay. Aunt Gizla. My nana and Aunt Gizla, they used to knit me socks. They called my little sister Katria and me Dearie. Everyone was Dearie. But I always put the socks on the wrong foot. That's on the wrong foot, Dearie. Into the storage room you go. Or they'd make me walk barefoot in circles like in the army, left, left, left, and then the other way, right, right, right, then into the storage room you go."

Dr. Enright frowned. "They locked you in the storage room? With socks? Without clothes? To learn left from right?"

"Usually in pyjamas. I'd get up in the morning and pull on my socks and come into the living room and if they were on the wrong foot, into the storage room you go. Dearie."

"Do knitted socks even have a left and right foot?"

"I think they do but I could never tell."

"So ... how do socks, clothes, and storage room relate to right now? Don't just come back with smartass attitude. Tie that together for me."

Renata slid back in her chair. She rested her chin on her chest in thought. Finally she said, "Every time I go to see my gynecologist — he's cute, like Bradley Cooper, thirty-five years old — in his office, I have to go into this room not much bigger than a closet and take off my clothes, all but my socks, and put on this hospital outfit. When I lean back in the examining chair, my feet up in the stirrups, his head between my legs, I feel like he's down there playing with his mouse, trying to see inside me, which is how you're making me feel, like you've locked me in your storage room and made me put on these hospital clothes and you're sitting there playing with your mouse trying to see inside me, and, Dr. Enright, it's pissing me off."

Dr. Enright was staring at her as though he was trying to decide into which checkbox this line of smartassery should fit. "I don't get it, Renata. Why did they put you in the storage closet?"

Renata thought a few moments, trying to remember the details. "My aunt Gizla, my dad's sister, and my nana were the same. If I wet the bed, they would tell me I was drinking too much water. You drink too much water, Dearie, so you must stay in the storage room in your pyjamas until you learn not to drink so much water. I never knew how much was too much until I wet my pants, like uh-oh, too much water. Aunt Gizla wouldn't let me change right away, so that in the morning she'd be sitting in her chair knitting the socks and she'd say, 'Don't come near me, Dearie, you stink. Into the storage room you go and spend the day in your own stink.'"

Renata leaned back in her chair and closed her eyes. "I'm sort of enjoying this, Doctor, tripping back to childhood. I'm sitting in this nice chair, eyes closed, picturing this little girl standing by Aunt Gizla's chair, soaking wet and stinking in her pajamas."

The doctor hesitated long enough for Renata to wonder what was going on. She opened her eyes just a crack. He was studying her, looking into her, it seemed.

He said, "Keep your eyes closed, like a minute ago, picturing yourself in wet PJs. You're five years old. Can you picture yourself?"

Renata pictured herself.

"Pretend you're in the storage room. Describe the storage room."

"It's too small for a bedroom, like a big walk-in closet, with a little window and a green curtain and a clock on the wall so we would know when we could come out."

"What else did you do that was wrong besides wetting the bed?"

Renata gave this question some thought. "You know what, Dr. Enright? I never knew. I thought the click-clack of the knitting needles through the storage room door was sending me messages to do something wrong so they could keep me in the storage room and not have to put up with me. My nana and Aunt Gizla did the same thing. They both had one-bedroom apartments with a storage room. Yeah, I see what you mean. They both sent me click-clack messages. Yeah, totally. I see what you mean. And they weren't just wee-wee messages."

"Describe these messages. Were they in words?"

"Clickety-clack, the sound of the knitting needless. I thought they were words but I couldn't understand them, or I thought I was losing them in the dark and my ears couldn't find them. They were on the storage room floor but I was afraid to try and find them because if I stepped on them, the words that is, I'd get in trouble for stepping on them with fresh-knitted socks."

"You said 'in the dark.' But the room had a window."

"Covered by a green curtain and I couldn't reach the light switch. That was on purpose so I couldn't study my spelling so then they could blame me for failing spelling and bam..."

"...into the storage room. And this was done by the aunt who died on the same day you jumped off the subway platform..."

Renata stared at him. "You're trying to trick me, aren't you?"

"I'm trying to evaluate you."

'To see if you can slide your mouse into the box labelled, what, aunt-killer?"

"To see if you need to be here."

"Like the psychiatrists evaluate pedophiles and say the child abuser is all better now, let him get a job in a daycare centre? But I've already got a job that you're keeping me from. Although, if you feed me those painkillers every day I might consider making this my home ... but no, probably not."

"Renata. This isn't a game."

Renata sat up in her chair. She closed her eyes. After what seemed like five minutes, sensing him staring at her, she took a peek. "Dr. Enright?"

"Yes, Renata."

"Why don't you have a couch for me to lie on?"

"This interview would go easier and quicker if you would stop playing games, Renata."

"Dr. Enright?"

"Yes, Renata."

Renata could feel sparkle coming into her day. Renata cocked her head, coyly, she hoped, and added a bit of a smile. She opened her bathrobe and slid down in her chair. "You're starting to look like Bradley Cooper, Dr. Enright. Would you and your mouse like to play gynecologist with me?"

Renata watched Dr Enright ride his mouse to the target and hit the checkbox. She said, "Is that a yes?"

"I don't think I have that checkbox on here, Renata."

"I know you're pretending to evaluate me, Dr. Enright. But I have an idea. I was wondering, in fact, Doctor, talking about your mouse gave me an idea. I don't need any help, but my little sister does. My older sister Emma and I have been trying to get Katria to go to a doctor but she won't go and she won't go to emerg and even if she'd agree to see a psychiatrist, there's a two-hundred-year waiting list. But here I have a bed in a mental hospital that I don't need and my little sister needs a bed in a mental hospital, especially now since our father, Comrade Ivan, poisoned Algernon, her mouse. I'm afraid she's going to do something crazy. So can we switch, make a trade, let my little sister have my bed?"

"It doesn't work that way."

"Is this some kind of mental hospital craziness? If the mental hospital has beds for the insane people and if the sane person has a bed and the insane person has no bed, which person should be in the insane bed?"

"Renata, be serious."

"Well, I am serious. This doesn't make sense. There's nothing wrong with me but I have a bed and there's something wrong with Katria and she can't have a bed. That's crazy."

"You're here for an evaluation to see if you killed your aunt Gizla."

Renata let out an exaggerated sigh. She closed her eyes and mouthed a one to ten. She said, "Dr. Enright. We both know you're cooking that report, twisting the facts, so you can keep me here in your storage closet for your own amusement, a cute young blonde in nightwear. I did not kill my aunt. I did not jump off the subway platform and my little sister is on a junk food revenge diet which is like committing suicide,"

"Revenge? Against whom?"

Renata threw up her hands "Oh boy. You're testing my patience. Revenge against Comrade Ivan who killed Algernon the mouse, and yes, as much as I'm enjoying this conversation and these pills, which were definitely a trip, I want to go. Tomorrow is Monday. I've got a full day of appointments."

Dr Enright made a note on his pad.

Renata opened her bathrobe and slid further down in her chair. "You're looking like Bradley Cooper again, Dr. Enright. Would you like to play Hide the Mouse with me?"

"Who are you right now, Renata? "

Renata paused her expression into a lingering smile for the doctor as she said, "The look on your face, a look which you might give yourself in the mirror while combing your hair before going on a date, checking that the part along the left, my right, is straight. Where's this look coming from? Have you been having urges while you've been playing with your mouse, like, you know, the urges the gynecologist gets?"

"Who are you right now, Renata?"

Renata pulled her bathrobe tight. "Who am I? I'm an airhead hairdresser. My interests are nice clothes, nice nails, nice hair, nice makeup. I have no interest in who is crazy and who isn't. I keep telling you … well okay, you want me to cooperate? Here's the sort of thing Aunt Gizla did to me: she put fig balls that looked like dogshit in my lunch."

Dr. Enright stared at her.

"Dr. Enright?"

"Yes, Renata."

"I wouldn't mind talking about fig balls. That really pissed me off, her doing that."

"Why?"

"In grade one, the kids traded desserts at recess. I couldn't trade. Nobody wanted a dessert that looked like dogshit."

"Why are you making these connections, Renata? Fig balls and dog excrement and gynecologists and couches and syphilis?"

Renata thought for a minute. "Yeah, totally, I see what you mean, and yeah, probably."

"Yeah probably what?"

Renata sagged in her chair. "I don't know, Dr. Enright. I have no idea. There must be a yeah probably in there somewhere; otherwise, you wouldn't have asked the question. But hmm … funny thing … I feel good talking about, you know … fig balls. I got a bad reputation from those fig balls and I did a lot of pointless snivelling about, you know, how those fig balls were ruining my life."

A tap-tap sounded on the office door. When the doctor called "Come in," Miss Jordan appeared. She handed Dr. Enright a note. He unfolded the paper and glanced at the message.

"A message from your sister, Emma. Your aunt Gizla's funeral has been delayed. The death is suspicious. They're doing an autopsy."

Dr. Enright checked his watch and wrote the time on his pad. "So, here's what I'd like you to do. Write a letter to Aunt Gizla and tell her how you feel about things. It's called writing a trauma narrative."

"And then can I go home?"

"We'll see."

"I don't think you can keep me, Dr. Enright. I'm only a hairdresser and not a very smart one at that, according to my father, but I think I can go home if I want."

"No, you can't. If you leave the police will bring you back. That's the law. You are as of now committed to a psychiatric facility. You're here until I say you can go".

CHAPTER EIGHTEEN

If Katria stood at the closed door of her bedroom and looked up, the door would swing open and her mother would come in. Sometimes Katria could see a light behind her, following her in. Sometimes Katria could see Moms sitting outside the bedroom door, waiting quietly, and as Katria went downstairs, her mother would follow along at her heels to wherever she was going. Sometimes, standing at the kitchen counter, Katria looked up and the door would swing open but there would be no one there, but then she'd go to the window and look out and she'd see Moms, waiting outside. Then after a while, Katria might see that door swing open again, and Moms would get up and come inside for a snack. Katria took pictures of each of these strange happenings with her cellphone, tip-toeing around quiet as a mouse, but her mother was in none of them.

But there in one of them, in a reflection in the glass of Comrade Ivan's bedroom window, holy gosh, was her mother's image, standing next to a rack of hanging clothes. This triggered something in Katria's brain, like a buzz in her ear from the invisible electronic umbilical wire, so Katria decided to look through the hanging clothes tucked away under the basement stairs. Way at the back Katria found the ribbed cinch midi dress her mother wore the day she got married. And on the floor in the back Katria found her mother's high-heels. And on a shelf Katria found a black bracelet and matching black necklace.

Katria had been looking up her mother's weight loss charts on Google. For the first few days in the coffin, she'd have gained weight. Then she'd have gradually been losing weight, maybe two pounds a day. Maybe more. So by now her mother would be, who knows, maybe one hundred pounds, the exact weight Katria was now.

Katria tried on the dress and, oh my god, it fit. If this wasn't a message from Moms then what was it? Almost as good as a direct phone call from the Mt. Hope Cemetery.

CHAPTER NINETEEN

Seven o'clock Monday morning, Emma opened her laptop and Googled "homicides by poison." She printed a copy, and highlighted while she drank her morning coffee:

- *The Tylenol Killer injected cyanide into Tylenol gel capsules, resealed the packaging, and put them back on the pharmacy shelf. Seven people died, no arrest was made.*

- *Urooj Khan died unexpectedly one day after the Illinois lottery issued him a cheque for $1,425,000. The standard toxicology test came back clear, so Khan's death was judged as heart disease because he was overweight. But the Khan family didn't buy the results. The coroner agreed to follow up with more tests and discovered Khan's blood was loaded with cyanide. The killer was his wife.*

- *The Curry Killer, Lakhvir Singh, killed her boyfriend by putting aconite derived from monkshood from his garden into his curry. She'd have gotten away with it but she didn't dispose of the leftover curry.*

- *George Henry Lamson killed his brother-in-law by putting aconite derived from monkshood from his garden into his birthday cake. Lamson didn't dispose of the leftover cake.*

- *Maggie McDonald poisoned her husband with aconite from the monkshood growing in her garden. While the husband lay on the floor gasping his final breaths, his wife watched a soap opera. When it ended, she finished him off with his hammer.*

Then Emma googled 'criminal poisoning with sodium fluoroacetate,' otherwise known as ten-eighty.

- *Developed by the Nazis, undetectable in an autopsy, with probable post-mortem diagnoses of a heart attack.*

- *Thought to be the perfect poison for Nazi death camp use but was later rejected because it was too dangerous for the inexperienced death camp guards to handle.*

- *Three siblings died in close order from heart failure in Oklahoma City. These deaths might have been ruled a genetic coincidence except for the fact the siblings were children. Forensics investigated further and found trace elements of some kind of poison sprinkled on the vanilla wafers the children had eaten. Forensics suggested that ten-eighty was the only poison lethal enough to kill with such a small quantity.*

- *Ten-eighty was suspected to be the poisoning agent in a rash of deaths by ventricular arrhythmias in a two-block area in Idaho Falls. According to the Post, since the chemical had been banned for decades, it must have been purchased and stored before the ban came into effect and was now being sold on the black market from Russia.*

- *Fifty-year-old minister S. S. Berrie had been married to Fannie Berrie for twenty-nine years. When Mr. Berrie got involved with his seventeen-year-old secretary, he gave Mrs. Berrie a lethal dose of ten-eighty in her orange juice. She died of heart failure within three hours. No autopsy was performed. Fifty-nine days after the death of his wife, Mr. Berrie married his secretary. Suspicious relatives notified police. A search of his house produced a half-empty package of ten-eighty which*

Mr. Berrie claimed he had used to kill raccoons living in his attic. A few days later Mr. Berrie produced a suicide note he said he found in his wife's bible. Handwriting analysis proved that this was not Mrs. Berrie's handwriting. Mrs. Berrie was exhumed but chemical testing of the vital organs produced no sign of poison.

Emma closed her laptop. As stupid as he was, Mr. Berrie walked. But, thought Emma, most murderers are stupid. Or, if they're smart, they make a tiny mistake, like feeding a goldfish, wrecking the knitting, and painting toenails black a few minutes before they leave the scene.

CHAPTER TWENTY

Renata had arrived on time. First she'd stared at him. Then she glanced at the pad and pencil on the right side of his desk and his laptop and mouse on the left side of his desk. Then she'd scanned the interview room. Bare walls, no pictures. Zero of everything, except the wall clock above the door. Then she'd asked, "Is this the same storage room as last time, Dr. Enright?"

"No, it isn't. But they're both the same."

She said, "There's something strange going on here. An enigma wrapped up in a conundrum. First of all, you cooked up this story about me jumping off the subway platform. Then you used the autopsy as an excuse to make another appointment so you can fantasize about being my gynecologist in this storage room called an interview room. And now Dr. Enright, look what you've done. You put me in a different storage room, which is the same as the other storage room, even the same clock hanging on the same wall. So, what you're doing is trying to take me back into my past by recreating my childhood storage room trauma."

Dr Enright looked up and glanced around. "Yes, both interview rooms are the same. But the reason we are using this one is the other interview room was taken."

"Then, holy gosh, why am I trying to figure out what's different?"

She leaned closer to examine his hair. "I've got it. I'm a hairdresser so I notice stuff like hair. I remember you parted your hair on your right, my left. I think I might be onto something, Dr. Enright. Today you've parted your hair down the middle."

"Well, I sometimes switch back and forth."

"That means you're having wet dreams of being my gynecologist. And I still think you'd make a good one, you'd be having way more fun than you're having here talking about fig balls with Renata. But you know what, Dr. Enright? Renata spends all day listening to the customers sitting in her chair. Renata watches them in the mirror. She knows what they're going to say before they say it. Renata has been watching you in her mirrors, Dr. Enright. She knows what you were thinking, sitting back in your chair, fondling your mouse as you poke about in the mind of this new patient, Renata, her blue eyes a little dull from the pain pills you've been feeding her, her lips pouty from the date rape pills you've been wanting to feed her. And the way she's brushed her wavy blonde hair into a sidesaddle ponytail that she, at just the right moment, you hope, will shake down over her shoulders. Here she sits, attractive and, I might add, sexy in that robe — skimpy thin PJs underneath, almost see-through — you're making her wear, five-foot-five, one-hundred-and-ten pounds, Russian descent, too bad the measurements are missing but I can get them from her and give them to you. But here's the question: which one of you, the doctor or the man, the mask or the face, the pencil or the mouse, will be writing those measurements down to take home when this, our last interview, is finished?"

"I'm the one who decides when our interviews will be finished."

"Well, as far as I'm concerned, we've talked about everything. But I have one question. Why do they call this place the Cathedral?"

"There used to be a cathedral on this piece of land. They tore it down and built the Monroe Institute on the original foundations."

"And the other mental facility?" said Renata. "They call it the Abandon."

"Same story. The original property was the Church of Saint Abadios."

"Is it true what I heard about the Monroe?"

"What did you hear?"

"There's a basement door that leads to a tunnel and the tunnel leads to the sewer system and all the psychiatric lifers are down there living in the sewer."

"Yes, that's true."

"The lifers live in the sewer?"

"Yes, they do."

"Do they have their clothes?"

"No, they don't. They have no privileges."

"Don't they get cold?"

"We give them blankets."

"What do they eat?"

"They have a working farm down there."

"There's no sunlight."

"They grow mushrooms."

"That's all they eat?"

"Well, they eat stuff from the sewer. Lots of good stuff in the sewer."

"Do they have children?"

"They have children. They have their own school system."

"Do they have lights? How can they read?"

"We run an extension cord from the nurse's station."

Frowning, lower lip pouting, Renata seemed to be puzzling through the logistics of this situation.

"You must think I'm stupid," she said

"Do you think you're stupid?"

"You can't run an extension cord all the way from the nursing station to a basement and through a tunnel and into the sewer system."

"Why not?"

Renata thought about it. "Maybe you could. Yeah. Totally. Why not. But kids shouldn't be allowed to grow up in a sewer."

"Why not? Do you think you grew up in a sewer?"

"I never said that."

"Yes, you did. Making up this story is your way of telling me that you feel like you grew up in a dark place with no sunlight and no clothes, only a blanket, with nothing to eat except food that looked like it came from a sewer."

She hesitated. She frowned an unblinking stare. "Which one of us is crazier do you think, you or me? The conversation you and I just had is about the same as the one I might have with a crazy person. A crazy person can't tell crazy from real. I know the conversation we just had was crazy, so I'm not crazy, and if I'm not crazy I shouldn't be here."

Dr. Enright pulled his chair closer to his desk. "Let's see what you've written in your trauma narrative."

She handed him the letter. "I wrote to Mary Carol."

"Who is Mary Carol?"

"The lady who gives knitting classes on the TV."

Her face was serious but he was sure she was kidding. He said, "I've never heard of, nor can I imagine, a knitting program on TV."

"My nana watched it. I didn't watch it with her. She locked me in the storage room so I wouldn't bother her while she was watching Mary Carol."

"What sort of 'bothering her' did you do to deserve to be put in the storage room?"

Renata studied his face. "Do you know what you just did? You phrased that question to make it my fault. I didn't do anything. So the question should've been, 'Why did she think you deserved to be locked in the storage room before you even did anything?'"

"Why did she think you deserved to be locked in the storage room before you even did anything?"

"I was something she didn't want."

"Why did she not want you?"

"I think you should get busy with your mouse on that one. Why did she not want me? Aunt Gizla did the same. Sometimes she made me hold my tongue with my finger and thumb like this—" Renata stuck out her tongue and held it with her index finger and thumb, her cheeks puckering into matching dimples. "Do you think holding my tongue caused damage? Would you like to examine it, Dr. Enright?" She stuck it out again. "See how the tip curls a little on each side? I think that's from holding it in the middle for half an hour at a time, longer if I let it go because then I'd have to start all over again."

"Hold it out." He squinted at her tongue but didn't get out of his chair to look closely. "I think it's all right, Renata. It doesn't seem to interfere with your ability to talk now."

"Not now. Not then. Because the damage that was done was not to the tongue."

"When you got locked in the storage room, did you protest? Stick up for yourself?"

"I always said 'I'm sorry.' And then I'd say, 'Mistakes shouldn't matter if you say you're sorry.' But Nana would say, 'Mistakes do matter. That's why they're called mistakes.'"

"Tell me about your other mistakes."

"How about I tell you about one of your mistakes? I just said the damage that was done was not to my tongue. You should have jumped on that."

"I'm the one deciding what should be jumped on."

"Ah, Doctor. 'Jumped on.' Freudian. Would you like me to help you with that?"

"Did your nana or your aunt Gizla ever apologize to you for this damage?"

Renata frowned at the question. "Of course not. My dad, Nana, my aunt Gizla, never. A Russian saying, 'Nikogda ne izvinyaysya': never apologize to anyone."

"Answer me this, Renata: what should've prevented Aunt Gizla and Nana from locking you in the storage room and making you hold your tongue?"

"I don't know. Children's Aid?"

"How about guilt?"

"They should've felt guilty for doing it."

"Do you feel guilty, Renata?"

"For what?"

"For anything."

"Not usually."

"Do you feel guilty for killing your aunt? Given what you've told me, she probably deserved it."

"And if I say no you'll direct that mouse to 'psychopath,' which is why you asked a leading question."

"Do you feel guilty for killing your aunt?"

"No."

"Why not?"

"Because I didn't kill her." Renata crossed one leg over the other. "Do you want me to read the letter?"

"Yes, please." He held it out to her.

But she didn't take it. She said, "You're moving on when you should be circling back to the big question. Why did she not want me?"

"Read the letter, Renata."

Renata shrugged. "You're the doctor." She took the letter and opened it. "Dear Mary Carol. Do you remember me? When Nana wasn't around, like in the bathroom, I'd phone you to complain about being locked in the storage room while she was watching the knitting show."

"Just Nana? Or Aunt Gizla too?"

"You're not paying attention. They were both the same. They both had a goldfish called Dr. Goldstein. They both had a dog called Rolfie. They both watched the knitting show. They both locked at me in the storage room. Sometimes they'd do one better and lock me in the closet in the storage room."

"What did Mary Carol tell you to do?"

"Stab them with their knitting needles."

Renata said this without anger, he noted. A violent act should bring with it a marked emotional response.

"Tell me this, Renata: did they lock you in the storage room so they wouldn't get stabbed while they watched the knitting?"

Renata shifted her eyes away and stared at the opposite wall. Then she placed her hands in her lap and imitated knitting gestures and finger movements. "If you rephrase the question to why did they lock you in the storage room I will tell you the answer."

"Why did they lock you in the storage room?"

"Knitting is a form of relaxation, Dr. Enright. One stitch at a time directed to some end, like a scarf or a sweater. But for Nana, it was obsessive compulsive. She had to do one hundred stitches in a row because that's how many times she'd been raped. Each stitch a stab of the needle, stab one, stab two, stab three: rapist one, rapist two, rapist three. When she reached one hundred, she had stitched herself back together and there would be no more rapes that day. Aunt Gizla had her own rapes and her own number that she used to block out or drive away or take control of the war demons, Dr. Enright."

She set the knitting aside, folded her hands, laid them in her lap, and waited for his answer.

"So they locked you in the storage room so you wouldn't interrupt the count."

"Yes."

"So the knitter, Nana, had knitted another knitter, Aunt Gizla."

"Yes."

"One stitch at a time and had she had children the knitted knitter would have knitted another knitter one stitch at a time."

"You asked me why they made me hold my tongue—" She lowered her eyes and stared at her hands. She seemed to be thinking about the idea. "Yeah. I definitely made them lose their count. I did that. And yeah, that's why I feel guilty."

She leaned back and heaved a sigh. "They had to be counting something to look as though they weren't counting, and they had to be knitting something in order to justify the knitting, so they knitted socks. So yeah, the behaviour makes sense to the one doing it."

"Let me guess, Renata. For knitting socks to make sense, someone had to wear them."

Renata smiled. "You nailed it, Doc. But you know what? Now that you've helped me understand why they locked me in the storage room, I feel much better and I think I'm ready to go home."

"But you have a lot of stored up anger, Renata."

Renata looked away. Her lips tightened. She sat up and pulled her robe tight around herself. "Me? Nah. I have no anger. I say to hell with it. I'm a party person."

"Renata. How are you dealing with your anger?"

She let her slippers fall to the floor. She pulled her bare feet up to rest on the rim of the chair and wrapped her arms around her knees, hugging herself and rocking like a child.

"Renata? How are you dealing with your anger?"

Startled, she looked at him, frowning, not understanding the question. Then she sat up straight and put on her slippers. She smiled a megawatt smile, white, straight, and perfect. She ran the tip of her tongue over her lips. "Holy gosh, Dr. Enright. I think you've hit on something."

He waited for what would come next.

"We're making big progress today, aren't we?"

"Indeed, yes."

"Indeed? You talk like the queen. A self-importance thing, Dr. Enright?"

"I guess."

Renata ran her fingers through her hair. She put her slippered feet on the floor and slid down on her spine. "Indeed. This is complicated stuff." She moved her hips from side to side to reposition herself.

Dr. Enright pretended to be occupied with his laptop, trying his best to not watch her intentional rearranging of her body, smoothing the robe down along her thighs so that it hung over the chair on either side of her legs.

Finally, to stop her display, Dr Enright said, "If I'm knitting a profile of Renata, then Renata is right now being knitted. What would you like me knit for this report as I sit here knitting Renata?"

She wiggled herself almost flat, barely covered by the bathrobe. "Is it time to have a serious talk with me, Dr. Enright?"

"Yes, it is. The brain remembers everything your nana and your aunt did to you and the brain keeps score. Now, in a safe situation of doctor-patient privilege in which you're fully in control, no need to hide, give me the words that I can write down, one stitch at a time, on this assessment to describe how Renata deals with her anger."

She stood up, opened her robe and refastened it around herself, then sat down again.

"All the time we've been talking, you've been squirming around in your chair with your robe open, flaunting your body. So the words you are giving me are 'Look at me now, sitting here half-naked, making you pant like a dog.'"

Renata stared at him, her usually Bambi eyes now an icy blue. She settled back in her chair. Her robe settled into a half-open position. "I'm feeling a lot better about everything. I had a lot of anger at you for trying to mess with my mind, but you've cured me of that, so I'm not going to kill Nana after all."

Dr. Enright checked the clock on the wall, something he didn't like to do because it was dismissive. But it was definitely time to end the session.

"I think in my report I will say that the knitter knitted another knitter and the two knitters knitted a very angry Renata. The abusive patterns from childhood are internalized and hidden by a persona, in your case a sexy party girl, except for when the negative feelings get released. To try and make a Renata-type personality accountable for her behaviour would result in destroying her persona, and defenses built up since childhood would crumble. But help is available for dealing with the repressed anger that made you kill your aunt Gizla. It is available right here in this hospital, where you are going to stay for the next little while. Your shadow self is Renata and you are Renata. You're both Renata. One is the sexy young woman, a carefree party girl polishing her sex-queen image. A smoke-and-mirrors charmer. The more votes she gets, the more she believes she's the person she's pretending to be. Until the other Renata steps in, hidden but never gone. Something from childhood gets triggered and the abusive core, the internalized abusing parent, will assert itself, like a safety valve letting off steam. Then, when the steam is reduced, the abusive valve closes, the persona emerges once again, and the shadow self is submerged once again."

"So in your report you'll say it was my shadow self that killed Aunt Gizla."

"And in my report, I'll say your shadow self will kill your nana and your father, and, by the way, what happened to that drug dealer character your report stated you were partying with the day you fell off the subway platform?"

Renata's eyes lowered and her shoulders slumped. She wiped away a tear. She got up and went to the door. Then she turned and with her megawatt smile said, "Do you know what, Bradley? All the time that you were trying to see inside me, you were playing with your mouse. You've ripped it right out of its port."

CHAPTER TWENTY-ONE

Katria was going through Renata's dresser drawers looking for clothes belonging to Moms when she found a short brown skirt and tight brown sweater belonging to Renata. Katria tried them on. If Katria wore a skirt that short and a sweater that tight Comrade Ivan would tell her to take it off and put on something decent. If he told Renata to put on something decent, she'd probably go shorter and tighter, hike the skirt right up to her underwear. "Renata, your skirt is too short!" Up goes the skirt. Sometimes up goes the finger. If Katria gave him the finger, she'd be grounded for life. But Renata was smarter than Ivan. Whatever he said she came back with a smartass comment that made him look stupid.

Then Katria found a skirt-blouse combination that Moms wore before she put on the weight. The skirt fit Katria pretty good, but it went down to her knees and the blouse buttoned up to her chin; it was more like something Emma would wear. But that was okay. Katria felt like Emma was her soul sister. She was easier to talk to than Renata, who would walk in the front door and plunk her long, bare legs down on Comrade Ivan's chesterfield, a towel needed, that's how short her skirts were, and half the time not even say hello.

Katria heard footsteps on the stairs. "Have you talked to him, Emma?"

"They've done the autopsy, so I think I will after the funeral. Well, it's not really a funeral if there's no one there. That's why he's upset, because you won't go. So since he's upset anyway, I might as well tell him after the funeral."

"So you'll tell him we're moving out?"

"Yes. That outfit looks good on you, by the way."

Emma left to meet Ivan at the funeral at two o'clock. To pass the time, Katria went up to her bedroom and lay down on her bed. Then she got up, took off Emma's outfit, and put on her mother's wedding dress. She drew her legs up so her kneecaps were touching and looked through the gap between her thighs, that's how skinny she was getting.

Beside her lay the new wool socks Nana had given her. Emma had told her, "Instead of lying on your bed doing nothing, take out all your knitted socks. Sit in your chair and unravel all the socks they knitted you. Because you can't wear them out. You could live to be a thousand and you wouldn't wear them out. It's like once you put them on your feet you can't take them off."

"The brown ones," Emma had said. "I had brown ones like that. They were softer than a cottontail rabbit until they got slipped onto my feet. And then my feet would start to sweat and the dye in the wool would turn my feet yellow."

"Unravel them and throw them away." Emma picked up Katria's foot and placed it on her knee. "After you're done, don't do anything with this foot that will bring back memories of socks. Go barefoot. No socks."

So, after Katria had unravelled the brown socks, she had taken the red socks from the dresser drawer and laid them on the kitchen table and sat down in the chair and stuck out her two bare feet while she unravelled the red ones.

Then Emma had explained about Big Steps. That's how she wrote it on her pad where she wrote stuff down.

- *Get your ears pierced. BIG STEP.*

- *Bring your boyfriend home to meet not Daddy but Emma. BIG STEP.*

- *Go to university. BIG STEP.*

Then she said, "I was afraid to take Big Steps because I remembered Aunt Gizla and Nana always put me in the storage room for doing even the little steps wrong. Where would I get put for doing a Big Step wrong? Into the closet in the storage room, I guess."

Emma explained about triggers, how one thought spurs on another. She set up dominoes on the kitchen table and said each one was a thought. Then she gave the first thought that was a right-now thought a gentle nudge. Katria watched the next thought that was standing there doing nothing wake up and come to life. It brought on the next thought and so on all the way back to grade three when the kids laughed at her for wearing homemade socks that sagged and bunched up around her ankles. And since she couldn't put them in the dryer, they never disappeared like ordinary socks.

Emma had told Katria, "When my mother left him, Ivan said, 'Emma, tell your mother if she doesn't come back in ten days I'm going to kill myself.' So every day from then on he said nine days left before I kill myself, eight days left before I kill myself, seven days left. It was, like, six days left before we go to Disneyland. I could hardly wait."

Still wearing the wedding dress, Katria climbed under the covers. She was thinking, Aunt Gizla died a week ago. All the undertaker had to do was drain the blood, pack her butthole with cotton, and lay her out in her coffin, and then the people come in and out to have a look, but that only takes about four days. But then, oh my gosh, they'd ordered an autopsy.

So now, because of the autopsy, she wasn't six feet under where she should be, starting to rot like she should be, the worms already enjoying the rhubarb like they should be. She was laid out on a gurney in a funeral parlour.

CHAPTER TWENTY-TWO

Dr. Enright motioned for Renata to take her usual chair. "Renata. At the end of our last session, I had a headache. Why is that, do you think?"

"Too much Starbucks?"

"Try again."

"You need brain surgery?"

"This session is starting with mind games. The last session ended with mind games, flirting for your amusement. Coquetry, it's called."

"Coquetry?" She put on an innocent look.

"You're doing it to throw me off balance. Why? I can tell you why. You are trying to derail my report by drawing me into silly mind games. You are turning my evaluation into a farce."

She put on a sorry look. "Yeah. I see what you mean."

"What is it that you see?"

No answer.

This was her fifth day in the hospital. She'd had lots of time to think about her situation. He said, "For my report, Renata, can I have, in your own words, why you killed Aunt Gizla?"

She kicked off her slippers, crossed her legs, and hugged her white hospital issue bathrobe around herself. "Nana and Aunt Gizla each had a goldfish called Dr. Goldstein. They both looked the same. They both had big eyes. I wondered if Dr. Goldstein was a drone surveillance camera. I know drones look more like big insects but I thought they could look like a goldfish with big eyes recording everything I did in the storage room so they could put me back in the storage room the minute I got out. They did that. Or Nana would tell Aunt Gizla the bad thing I did and Aunt Gizla would put me in her storage room the next day. They alternated days. I asked Aunt Gizla if Nana locked her in the storage room when she was little. She pretended not to know what I was talking about. She said, 'You're a lucky little girl. And I'm not locking you in a storage room. I'm suggesting you have some quiet time in the spare bedroom. That's where you have a quiet time.' And I said, 'But this room is where you store stuff. It's a storage room. It's a bedroom. And I can't come out—' And she'd say, 'No you can't come out until I tell you.' And I'd say that I didn't want to be in the bedroom which was really a storage room. And she'd say, 'Well, you need quiet time and you need to be more cooperative or we'll put you in foster care and you'll get a good swat…'"

Dr. Enright wrote a note on his pad: She's switched her childhood memories into present time. Keep her there. Then he said, "So, you're in the storage room. What do you do in there with Dr. Goldstein?"

She looked up, startled.

"What do you do in there with Dr. Goldstein?"

"I talk to Dr. Goldstein. I told you that."

"Why do you like to talk to Dr. Goldstein?"

"Talking to my aunt Gizla or my nana is the same as talking to a doorknob. But when I talk to Dr. Goldstein, he looks right at me with his big round eyes and he listens. When I'm finished talking, he opens and shuts his mouth as though he's talking back to me."

"What is Dr. Goldstein saying? You're seven, eight years old, talking with Dr. Goldstein. What is he saying?"

"He wants me to teach him to ride a bicycle so we can run away together."

"Are you hearing Dr. Goldstein saying that right now?"

"Dr. Enright?"

"Yes, Renata?"

"Do you think I'm stupid?"

"Why would you ask that?"

"Because your next question will be, 'Did Dr. Goldstein tell you to kill Aunt Gizla?'"

"Did he?"

Renata uncrossed her legs. She slipped down in her chair. The bathrobe opened, revealing the PJ top two buttons undone.

"After Aunt Gizla died, what do you think happened to Dr. Goldstein?"

"I think my father flushed him down the toilet."

"Like he poisoned the mouse."

"Yeah, totally."

"He likes to kill things, it seems."

She reached out and nudged his arm. "You silly man. For Aunt Gizla to still have the Dr. Goldstein I talked to when I was seven, he'd have to be about fifteen years old."

She sat back in her chair, scowling, remembering something it seemed.

"Oh my gosh, Dr. Enright. Yeah, totally."

"Yeah totally what?"

"I just caught your internalized shadow self looking at my open PJ buttons."

"I was looking at your necklace, something you shouldn't have. I'm making a mental note to inform Miss Jordan."

Renata leaned forward, offering him a better look at the necklace. "Do you ever get the feeling you're on the wrong side of the desk, Dr. Enright?"

"Why would I?"

She placed her elbows on her knees. She smiled. She cocked her head to her left side and ran her fingers through her hair. She uncrossed her legs, opening her robe to reveal the slice of bare skin between the top and bottoms of her white hospital-issue PJs.

"Dr. Enright?"

"Yes, Renata."

"Why don't you have a couch in here for me to lie on? We could practice some coquetry while we're waiting for the police to come for me."

"There's no room."

"Do you have a couch in your office at the Abandon?"

"I don't have an office at the Abandon, but I'll have one at the new facility. They've bought the property belonging to the Church of the Ascension."

"They'll tear it down and build another mental hospital?"

"Yes."

"So all the churches are being torn down and replaced with mental hospitals?"

"It looks like it."

"And all the priests replaced with psychiatrists?"

"It looks like it."

"And all the bible study groups replaced with therapy groups?"

"It looks like it."

"And the parishioners will be called patients?"

"I guess so."

"Church of the Ascension … I bet the new place will be called the Erection."

"Probably."

"They make pills now to give men erections. Like eating disorders, personality disorders: erection disorders."

"So I've heard."

"Will the psychiatrists be able to abuse the patients like the priests abuse the parishioners?"

"I hope not."

Renata frowned. She lowered her head, apparently slipping deep into thought, trying to understand the question. She brought one hand up to the side of her face. "Holy gosh! Dr. Enright?"

"Yes, Renata."

"Every so often you hit the nail right on the head. That little voice in my head. Yes, I hear it."

"What does it say?"

She sat up. "I've got one for you. One day I was sitting with Aunt Gizla at the table. I watched her face. I began to see that she was transforming into her internalized shadow self. The jawline was the same, the look in the eyes the same, and the tilt of the head the same, but the face, which was usually hard, became harder and suddenly all those features of her mother that had hardened into permanence because of her old age — that's what happens, frowns and scowls and stuff age into permanence — all of sudden Aunt Gizla's features changed into the hardened features of her mother, and right there before my eyes Aunt Gizla became the internalized shadow self of, you guessed it: Nana."

"So then I began to pay more attention to how it happened. The right hand would come up to her right ear and she'd rest her head against her hand. Her left hand would come up to her chin and in this position, head lowered, she'd stare down into the tabletop for a few seconds, and then she'd straighten up and pick up on a conversation not related to what we'd been talking about but a new line of thought and I knew that some other person that was waiting in the shadows, namely her mother, my nana, had appeared."

"And then what?"

"She'd look over at me and say 'Renata? Renata?' as though she'd gone into some other reality and, coming back, didn't know for a moment who she was. She'd say 'Renata? Renata?' as though she was drifting in and out of now."

"So I'd play this game, Dr. Enright." Renata leaned both elbows on his desk and covered her face with her hands and peeked at him through her fingers. She lowered her head and brought one hand up to the side of her face. Her fingers strayed to her ear lobe and she looked at him and asked, "Is that you, Aunt Gizla? Or is that your internalized shadow self, Nana?"

Renata slid back in her chair, the robe now hanging off her shoulders. "These PJs are kind of tight across the chest. Did you pick them out specially for me, Dr. Enright, or was it your internalized shadow self?"

"The nurse picks them out."

Renata stood and removed her bathrobe completely. "It's too small. See? I can hardly do it up." She threw back her shoulders, then abruptly sat again.

Dr. Enright closed his eyes. He leaned back in his chair, his eyes closed tight. "You are intentionally wasting my time, Renata."

"Try rephrasing that question. Try why are you intentionally wasting my time?'

"Why are you intentionally wasting my time?"

"Because, Dr. Enright. Here you are with me in your storage room talking nonsense about a goldfish and erections. The last session in your storage with me we talked nonsense about living in the sewer system." She leaned forward. "I've been patient with you; I guess that's why you call us patients, we have to be patient. And I would have cooperated. But you locked me in your storage room. In my PJs. You shouldn't have done that. Not my jar of jam. You've pissed me off. Just like when I was locked in Nana's or Aunt Gizla's storage room, the only way to pass the time was to talk nonsense to Dr. Goldstein. Now here I am talking nonsense to a different Dr. Goldstein. Funny thing, just like there were two Dr. Goldsteins that looked the same, there are two Dr. Enrights that look the same, the one that's trying to look into me and the one that is pretending to not be trying to look into me. Do you know how I know? The more excited your shadow self gets, the more excited your mouse gets. See? You've pulled it out of its port again."

Dr. Enright sighed. He rubbed his forehead, surprised that the headache had taken so long in coming.

"Will you pick up your telephone, Dr. Enright, please?"

"Why?"

"I want to phone you. It's sort of anonymous, you know, you can tell someone something on the phone and leave a message when you can't do it face to face, it's like you're admitting to something without needing to identify yourself. Pretend I'm sitting here but it's my internalized shadow self is finally coming out. It's going to tell you something."

Dr. Enright picked up the telephone and put it to his ear. "Hello Renata."

Renata put her thumb to her ear, her little finger to her mouth, and whispered, "When I was fifteen, I had a boyfriend. He had an erection almost the whole time we were together. I did that to him. Have I done that to you, Dr. Enright? That's why you sit behind a desk playing with your mouse writing that Freudian nonsense on your laptop. Do you know what my father calls me? You have to write it down: The Cock Whisperer."

Into the telephone Dr. Enright said, "Did Dr. Goldstein tell you to kill Aunt Gizla because she locked you in the storage room?"

Renata's face softened into a coy smile. "Just once. One time. But I knew that was bad. So do you know what I did, Dr. Enright?"

"No."

"Guess."

"I can't."

"I turned the fishbowl the other way so, you know, he had his back to me, so I couldn't see his face to see what it was telling me."

"Did that help?"

"Yes. But Aunt Gizla noticed I had turned Dr. Goldstein with his back to me and she turned him around the way he was supposed to be. Everything had its exact spot and if I moved something, I got into trouble, into storage you go."

...

When his office hours ended, Dr. Enright usually drove straight home, although since he was not married, had no significant other, as they called it, home was no more than a two-bedroom condo in Etobicoke. Today he drove to the Office of the Coroner on Morton Shulman Avenue.

Each time Dr. Enright visited Dr. Bornstein, he seemed to have grown older. His hairline had receded further, his paunch had expanded, and his shoulders had narrowed. He reminded Dr. Enright that no one stays young forever. And no one stays attractive to the opposite sex for very long. For Dr. Enright, Plan A had been to start thinking about a relationship at thirty. Plan B had been to start thinking about a relationship at thirty-five. Plan A and B had come and gone and he hadn't even had a girlfriend. What was Plan C? Buy a sports car?

Dr. Enright said, "Renata, an attention-seeking charmer, a manipulator hiding behind a life of the party persona. Underneath the persona is the shadow self, a self-serving liar full of repressed childhood trauma whose existence she knows of but will never admit to."

Dr. Bornstein was sitting forward, his elbows on his desk, turning his pen end to end with the fingers of his right hand as he glanced through the report. He shrugged. "Her aunt died from a heart attack."

"Renata hates her aunt. A stroke can be murder. Selenium, thallium, cyanide, dimethyl selenide, all end in pulmonary edema. Their father is in the animal control business, poisons rats, mice, raccoons. What if Renata used her father's poison on her aunt?"

"Easily traced in an autopsy. If there was evidence of poison, we'd have found it."

"What if she used a poison that wouldn't be picked up in an autopsy?"

Dr. Bornstein leaned back in his chair and considered this possibility. "I'm old enough to recall the Nazis used an untraceable poison called fluoroacetate in Auschwitz. But it's been banned worldwide."

"That doesn't mean it's not still around, does it?"

Dr. Bornstein became thoughtful. He almost certainly had a relative who had died in Auschwitz. He said, "Your conclusion is a traumatized child gets even. I don't think so, not from what I see on this evaluation. The world is full of adults from traumatized childhoods."

"Until they get tipped over the edge and get a thought in their mind, and then, like Renata, add drugs and alcohol and they run with it."

Dr. Bornstein folded his arms and leaned further back in his chair. The sunlight through the window behind him revealed the thinness of his hair along the top. He said, "The autopsy results came through. There was no murder. This girl was inebriated. She fell off the subway platform. She should be discharged."

CHAPTER TWENTY-THREE

She hadn't thought that Aunt Gizla would collapse in her own all-you-can-eat nuclear-red rhubarb puke on the bathroom floor. But the floor was tiled, there were all kinds of cleaners under the sink, there was a change of clothes in the closet. She threw the pukey clothes into a plastic bag, cleaned her up, and laid her out on the floor in the storage room. She thought maybe she should lay Aunt Gizla's bible there beside her, in case, in a dying breath, Aunt Gizla wanted to ask Jesus for forgiveness for the way she had treated them. But no, Jesus rose again from the dead after three days, so forget the bible idea. Don't give Aunt Gizla any ideas about rising again.

First she had painted Aunt Gizla's toenails black. Then, with Aunt-Gizla correctness, she'd rinsed the vodka glass and placed it upside down in the sink. Then, with Aunt-Gizla incorrectness, she'd unravelled the knitting and bent the needles. Then, with Aunt-Gizla correctness, she'd fed Dr. Goldstein two pinches of fish food. Two pinches, Dearie. No no, no bigger pinches. But my fingers are too little. Too little? Nonsense. And look, you've spilled on the carpet so now you have to vacuum and not just where you spilled, the whole carpet and then a good swat and into the storage room you go.

She was at the door, ready to leave, when oh my god, there Aunt Gizla lay, looking kind of loopy, lying on the floor with her cellphone upside down in her right hand. Holy gosh. She had somehow managed to dial 911. And then, holy gosh, the coroner had wanted an autopsy. But, in the end, that had worked out okay. Into the underground storage room Aunt Gizla had gone.

The container for the ten-eighty had to be small enough to fit into her jacket pocket. She wandered up and down the aisle of the supermarket and finally decided on a small jar of mustard. More appropriate than jam. She paid for it and then walked a block to McDonald's and went into the washroom and scooped out all the mustard and rinsed it clean. Then she walked another two blocks to Walmart for more black nail polish.

After her four o'clock Mary Carol program, Nana always set aside her knitting and sat down on the living room chesterfield for two glasses of vodka, pronounced "wodka," before dinner. Russian custom. On Saturdays, instead of watching the knitting, she turned on the TV to watch the afternoon Hallmark movie. It was always about good people overcoming tragedies. Nana had just turned on today's movie about a doctor and a nurse. In a Hallmark doctor movie, they would not take off their clothes and do it on the floor of the doctor's office. They would do things like helping old people with no money get long-term care.

Nana eased her short, fat self into her easy chair. She looked like a Russian peasant woman: plain dress, plain grey hair in a bun, a round face with wire-rimmed glasses. She said, "Make me a wodka, Dearie."

"Tell me something, Nana, why is Dr. Goldstein on top of the television instead of in the storage room? Do you want me to put him in his proper place so he'll be there waiting for you?"

"Can you make me a glass of wodka, Dearie? A wodka and pickle."

"Don't call me Dearie. I'm not five years old anymore. But I guess on your last day on planet Earth you can call me Dearie."

She went into the kitchen. After pouring the half-tumbler of vodka she took out the mustard jar. She scooped out half a teaspoon of the ten-eighty and poured it into the glass. Then she opened the refrigerator and got a pickle.

Nana held the glass and stared at the clear liquid. Dearie thought, Uh oh, is some of the powder floating on the surface? But no, ten-eighty is a salt. Salt doesn't float. And Nana's eyesight is too weak to see anything, even if it could float.

Nana brought the glass to her mouth and took a careful sip. She set down the glass and returned to the television. She picked the glass up again for another sip.

"Why did you move Dr. Goldstein into the storage room?" Nana asked.

"So he'd be there waiting for you." Dearie settled into the .chair opposite Nana. "You're not drinking it right. It's down the hatch. Even Miss proper Gizla did it down the hatch. 'That's crude,' she'd say to me, when I did a down-the-hatch with my milk. But you've never been one to worry about being crude, know what I'm saying, Nana?"

Paying no attention, Nana drank it all in one gulp, down the hatch. "That's the way you drink in the old country. Before the Commonists." She took a bite of her pickle. "Get me another wodka, Dearie."

"If you apologize for putting me in the storage room, I'll get you another wodka."

"Why would I put you in the storage room?"

"I never knew, like I was a canary. The canary doesn't know why it gets put in the coal mine."

Nana fanned the air with her hand.

"That's like in a movie I saw, you fanning the air like that is the sign of a demonic presence that turns the fan of the air into the howling of the wind as before my eyes I watch your toenails turn from pale of day to black of night."

Nana held out the glass.

Dearie got up and took the glass to the kitchen and came back with a refill, the ten-eighty added. The first must be working through Nana's bloodstream already, she thought, the poison must be coursing through her veins. She handed Nana the drink and sat on the chair opposite, leaning forward in anticipation, like watching one of those undead characters, needing a place to sleep, climb into a coffin. First, he'd tap-tap on the lid and then he'd stand back, because if there was another body in that coffin, all the vacuum-sealed gas might explode into fire…

Nana gave the drink one sip and then down the hatch it went.

"It's a poison that causes heart failure, Nana. The heart failure you gave me by picking on me all the time can't be traced and the heart failure I'm giving you can't be traced."

Nana leaned her head against the chair back and closed her eyes.

"What heart failure? you ask. I know you still don't get it. Remember breakfast? Make me a slice of toast, Dearie, and then holy gosh I'm in the closet in the storage room for buttering the toast on the wrong side."

Nana was staring into her empty glass.

"You didn't eat your pickle."

"Is there anything wrong with this wodka?"

"What heart failure? you ask. Remember Children's Aid came and asked you about locking me in the storage room? 'I didn't lock her in the storage room,' you said to the Children's Aid people. 'She's a little liar.'"

Nana tried to get up, probably to take her glass out to the kitchen and rinse it under the tap and turn it upside down in the sink.

"Let me help you, Nana. Into the storage room you go."

But Nana collapsed back into her chair

"Get up out of your chair so you can drop dead on the storage room floor. I want to watch. I'm going to laugh so hard I won't be able to call the ambulance. In fact, I'll be laughing so hard they'll think I'm a lunatic on the loose and they'll hear me all the way to emergency and send the ambulance without me calling them."

Nana managed to get out of her chair and stumble into the storage room.

"Do you know what made me finally decide to do it? Remember that woman who stabbed her husband? Her husband was beating her up and she stabbed him one night with the scissors, imagine that, with the scissors she used to cut his hair! All the time she was snip-snipping she was thinking stab-stabbing. He bled to death on the living room floor while she sat in the chair laughing. Or maybe she was laughing at the television program. Not only did she get off, but also, she was a hero. I don't want to be a hero, and no one will know anyway. But I'll be a hero to me. A serial hero. First Gizla and now you and next Comrade Ivan."

Nana collapsed on her back on the floor of the storage room. "Have you got a drink of water?" she whispered, "Please, Dearie, a drink of water."

"Yeah, somewhere I do in fact, I think I've got a whole tap full of water. Why? Aren't you feeling well? Remember the time I asked you where the water comes from? You handed me the glass of water and you said it came from the toilet. 'It goes around from the toilet to the tap to the toilet.' You told me that so I'd stop drinking water so I'd stop peeing my pants. You drew a picture to show me how the water went from the tap to my stomach to my bladder to the toilet to the tap to the glass. So, no water for you, Nana. I don't want you to pee your pants."

Somehow Nana managed to sit up. She reached out to clutch the wall as she sank back on the floor.

Dearie wiped the prints off the glass and off the refrigerator and the cupboard and the knife and the pickle jar and whatever else she could think of. She thought, "Don't get sick, Nana. Just die without making a mess."

But Nana died so quick she didn't have time to get sick. Dearie couldn't help smiling a little as she intentionally spilled on the floor half of the Dr. Goldstein's two pinches of food. Socks for the Church Relief Basket, it said on the pamphlet next to the socks for the Inuit children whose parents didn't lock their kids in the storage room. She bent Nana's knitting needles from straight to crooked and unravelled the socks from knitted to unknitted. She painted Nana's toenails black and left.

CHAPTER TWENTY-FOUR

Emma phoned Renata. "Nana's apartment super said at eleven o'clock he walked by her door and heard the television was still on. Nana goes to bed at nine o'clock. At twelve, he walked by again and listened at the door and knocked. He let himself in. He found her on the floor in the storage room. Dead."

Emma heard Renata sip on something, this early in the morning probably coffee, before she said, "Well, she was old."

"I asked the super the first thing that came to me: 'Was her knitting pulled apart and were the needles bent?' The super said she must have had it in her hand when she got the heart attack and she went spastic and ripped it all apart."

"Makes sense."

"The second thing I asked, 'Did you notice if she'd just fed the goldfish? There'd be food floating in the water.' He said he didn't notice the goldfish."

Renata was silent, indifferent it seemed, sipping her coffee.

"The third thing I noticed when I arrived at Nana's was her toenails were painted black."

Renata's reaction was immediate. "Oh my god, like Aunt Gizla? What about Rolfie?"

"Rolfie is fine."

Renata was slow to answer. Finally, she said, "It's Katria. She said she was going to poison Aunt Gizla's Rolfie but not Nana's."

"It's not Katria. It's Ivan, using a banned poison called ten-eighty. He's the dog poisoner. He killed Aunt Gizla and her Rolfie and now Nana but not Nana's Rolfie to make it look like Katria."

Renata was silent, sipping her coffee. Finally, she said, "Nana has money stashed away and Ivan needs money. But if she died from ten-eighty they would know at the hospital, right? If the heart attack was from the poison?"

Emma cleared her throat before repeating what she'd learned about ten-eighty. Renata listened, sipping her coffee, or maybe she'd switched to vodka.

"So, what you're saying, Emma, is if you gave ten-eighty to a person there would be no trace in the blood or anywhere else? Skin analysis, hair analysis, all negative?"

"It's Ivan. Join the dots. He's the dog poisoner. Join the dots."

"What's your proof for the dog poisoner thing?"

"He's a meticulous nitpicker, which means he writes everything down. When I checked his receipts book, I found several $5000 bat calls. Bats live in attics all winter until June and July, when the baby bats start to explore. They come down through the walls and get disoriented and come out wherever they can find a hole. They can flatten themselves down as thin as a dime and come out at a light fixture. This is September. Bats are already settled for the winter, in the roof rafters upside-down sleeping off the summer, not bothering anyone. If he's not being paid these big bucks for getting rid of bats in the fall, what's he really getting paid to get rid of?"

Emma could hear the tinkle of ice cubes. Renata had definitely switched to something stronger. "So he's charging big money to catch them when they're hanging upside down in the rafters, remove them, and release them elsewhere."

"Maybe. But if anyone checked his books, they'd know releasing them this time of year would be killing them, which is illegal."

"So is killing dogs."

"You have to understand Ivan. He's a rigid rule-freak except when it suits him not to be. When I looked up addresses given on the high-expense bat bills, they were phoney. I checked with the Humane Society. The dates of the bats were the same as when the dead dogs were reported. So, then I looked up printing expenses for publishing and promoting his diet books. Join the dots. He's poisoning dogs to pay for his books."

"Maybe."

"Why maybe? Men like to kill things. Men buy guns and kill rabbits and deer and moose. Men start wars and kill women and kids. Men molest children and rape women. Men do all kinds of revolting things. That's the way men are. Just because you don't like the truth, doesn't mean it's not true."

Renata gave a heavy sigh as if she were sitting down with another needed drink. "You're right. I nearly got blamed for Aunt Gizla. I'm feeling sensitive. So why am I protecting him? I'm not: I'm getting scared."

"One other question, and this is a strange one. Did Ivan sometimes wear black toenail polish?"

"Ivan? Are you kidding?"

"But how would you know? Have you seen him in bare feet?"

Emma pictured Comrade Ivan sitting at his kitchen table painting his toenails black.

"Don't think so."

"One other question. Think about feeding Mr. Goldstein, Renata. When you stand over the bowl, what does a goldfish do?"

"Wag its tail?"

"No, seriously, what does it do?"

"Is this like a knock-knock joke?"

"No, it's not a joke. Have you ever fed a goldfish?"

"Yes, I have."

"So what does it do?"

"It looks up at you waiting for the food, wagging its tail."

"What kind of food?"

"Bird seed?"

"Forget it. Doesn't matter."

CHAPTER TWENTY-FIVE

Emma drove to Nana's three-story red-brick apartment building on Avenue Road. She found the superintendent in his apartment on the first floor watching television. He had an enormous belly, heavy features, and a suspicious face. But Emma's driver's license identified her and got her into Nana's apartment, escorted by the super's wife, a pear-shaped woman with a pleasant smile.

Emma hoped she'd leave her alone long enough to snoop, but she didn't. Didn't matter, for the clue Emma wanted was there in front of her on the little table by the chair: the knitting was unravelled, the needles bent.

Emma imagined herself sitting in the easy chair of her living room, knitting. She imagined sunshine streaming in one window, the knitting needles gliding through her fingers. She asked the super's wife, "Did your granny knit when you were a little girl?"

"My mother liked to knit. I'd wake up at midnight and there she'd be, knitting her way through her problems. She was always halfway through something, a scarf, whatever, not a day her needles were idle. The day she died her knitting was there in her lap as if she had just put it down and died."

"Would a knitter ever attack her knitting do you think, rip it apart and bend the needles?"

The super's wife was running her fingers along the living room wall, looking for something it seemed, not paying attention.

Emma continued, "Knitting is therapy, like yoga. You can go to the store and buy a pair of socks for less than the cost of wool."

"Therapy. Good point. My mother was a single parent. In the middle of a sleepless night, she knitted herself back together, ready for the next day of three bratty kids."

"If the knitting stitches you back together, the ripping would tear you apart."

The wife moved to the next wall, bothered by something, it seemed.

Emma persisted. "Knitters must like patterns and repetition, the same movement repeated again and again." And then, one thought following the next, Emma said, "Like the snip-snip of scissors, the movements repeated again and again."

"When is the son coming back? He painted this room without first taking off the wallpaper."

Emma persisted. "The day she died. Did she have any visitors?"

"I met a blonde girl, about twenty, in the hall, but I don't know what apartment she was coming from."

"Long hair, sort of curly, sexy dresser?"

"They're all sexy dressers. There's a Catholic high school around the corner. The fifteen-year-old girls, my husband calls them hookers in training, wiggling past his front window every morning on their way to school. Twinkies I call them, walking by with their skirts hiked up to their underwear."

Emma wandered into the kitchen. She noticed the rinsed glass in the sink was placed upside down. It was the same size of glass placed the same way as in Aunt Gizla's sink. Emma remembered this upside-down Boscov rule. If she could remember all the other rules, she could match the behaviour to the exact Boscov. Placing the victims in the storage room would apply to Katria and Renata. The upside-down-in-the-sink would apply to Ivan, but both Renata and Katria would go out of their way to break that rule, just as both Katria and Renata would go out of their way to wreck the knitting and bend the needles while Ivan would not, although Ivan could have wrecked the knitting and bent the needles to frame Renata and Katria…

Around in circles.

Emma searched the bedroom closets but could find nothing of interest. She did, however, without the super's wife noticing, slip the knitting and the glass into her jacket.

Emma walked across the street to where a short stout man was in his driveway arc welding the custom steel tube bumper of a pick-up truck.

Emma said, "Did you happen to see a white van in front of the building across the street yesterday?"

The man turned off the blowtorch and stood, removing his goggles. "Not that I remember."

Although he looked Italian, he didn't have an accent — second or third generation. He said, "I noticed a kid poking around looking for his cat. I told him we got cats wandering around all over the place. They call them urban roaming cats. Urban roaming cats, for fuck's sake. I said to the kid, See this bumper here? This is my uncle's pick-up. Every time he sees a cat on the road he swerves to hit it. He says he's run over so many cats his ten-year-old granddaughter calls them speed bumps because every time he sees one, he speeds up. His wife says to stop running over cats, so he says it's not his fault. They're attracted to his bumper because they got iron deficiency. He tells her he's driving along, listening to his gospel station, and here comes a cat galloping right at him, straight into the bumper. He says, I've got a buddy. He says the same thing. He says the urban cats at the gun range have a lead deficiency. When he's out practicing at the target over there, then from over here comes a cat and jumps right in front of the bullet."

Emma thanked him for his time and said if she needed a new bumper or needed some cats run over, she'd be back. She turned to leave but hesitated. "Did you maybe notice a blonde girl, long hair in curls, come out of the building?"

"That I did, well, maybe, I was wearing these goggles, hard to pick out details."

"You'd have taken your goggles off for this one."

He shrugged. "I was doing my work."

CHAPTER TWENTY-SIX

Katria woke up at four o'clock in the afternoon. She went downstairs and stood at the living room window waiting for Emma to return. Katria wasn't wondering what Emma and Ivan were saying. She wasn't imagining how angry he would be. She wasn't thinking about any of these things. She was thinking that the same poison that killed raccoons and skunks and whatever else Comrade Ivan poisoned had put Aunt Gizla and Nana into that same category: rodents, all of them. Ha! One dead rodent to the other, welcome to rodent heaven, Aunt Gizla. Here, let me get the door for you. Nana, welcome to rodent heaven. Here, let me get the door for you.

Katria left the window and went into the bathroom and stared at her mother's reflection. She climbed onto the scale. One hundred pounds from top to bottom, stubby arms and legs thick as stove pipes now thinned down top to bottom skinny as sticks, just like Moms.

Katria said to Moms, If Comrade Ivan won't let me paint my toenails black like yours, what am I supposed to do, sit in my chair all day and look at my hands, folded palms up in my lap, with nothing in them? Or should I ask you to put the black toenail paint in my hands and you'll do my toenails with the little brush. What do you think, Moms?

Well Katria, I remember the first time I painted my friend's toenails. It was summer and it was about two hundred degrees and I was sixteen and my girlfriend was sixteen and I painted her toenails and she painted my toenails. We were both wearing sandals. When we sat on the bed and looked down at our feet, our toes looked like rose petals. The rose petals were still on her toes the last day I saw her. So I wouldn't cry when she left, I concentrated on my rose petals. After that, every time I thought of her, I thought of the ten rose petals, and once a week I painted my toenails into rose petals. But when I married Ivan, he said no more painting toenails, and it felt like my rose petals had been peeled away piece by piece, like leaves turning brown and blowing away, and all that were left were my bare feet.

From her purse, Katria took out the bottle of black nail polish. She thought, It's a good thing you're not a guy, Moms. If you were, we couldn't do this. Take off your socks. I know. I know. Don't worry about Ivan. I'll put your socks back on when I'm done.

I didn't know any of your girlfriends, Moms, but you were my girlfriend and that's why I have those rose petals inside me, each one carrying a rose-coloured memory of trips to the zoo and rose-coloured memories of shared secrets. Stuff Ivan wouldn't let us do or have. That's how I try to remember you, by all the stuff he wouldn't let us do.

Katria stood by the front door to wait for Emma's return. She'd been gone a long time, but Katria was feeling hopeful. She was certain Emma would put Comrade Ivan out of their life for good. Guaranteed Gone. Katria had faith in Emma, but not in Renata. Renata was not to be trusted. Emma and Katria, they could feed Comrade Ivan some Guaranteed Gone, gone like Sunday dinner, pull the flusher and down into the sewer he goes. Katria liked to stare at him floating on the water in her puke as she pulled the lever. Ha. Let me get the door for you.

Emma's car pulled up, the white van right behind it. Ivan was dressed in his suit, looking ridiculous, like a car salesman, except he wasn't wearing a tie and his hair was too short. What did the priest say about Nana? Ha. She's on the way to Rodent Heaven. Let me get the door for you.

Emma and Renata started up the walk but Ivan drove off. Katria listened to Renata's high heels tap-tap along the sidewalk and watched her long legs and short skirt climb the porch steps. Katria knew that after she put Ivan out of her life, she'd go back to having normal legs like Renata, not sausage blobs, and not sticks, normal.

"What have you decided?" asked Katria.

"Katria!" Renata said. "What are you wearing? Whose is that? My god, Katria. That was Moms's favourite outfit."

Katria asked, "Why did he leave? I've been waiting."

Renata seemed stunned. "What do you mean waiting?"

"Surprise! I'm back!"

Emma said, "Katria is dressed for the occasion. Like me, dressed in plain black, like a proper widow." She turned to Katria. "Renata told Ivan he should move out. He said it's his house and he's not moving. So, sweetie, you and I are going to move. It's all worked out. Let's you and I go upstairs and change."

Emma took Katria's hand and they started up the stairs.

Renata, who had been following one step behind, said, "Katria, for goodness' sake, get a grip. Neither you nor I have any good feelings about either Gizla or Nana or Ivan, but for God's sake take off Moms's dress.

CHAPTER TWENTY-SEVEN

Renata stopped off at The Cutting Corner. She stood at the mirror, and skillfully dabbed a bluish smudge on her cheek. I should be a makeup artist in Hollywood, she thought. Not cutting hair in Toronto. That's what they said about me in the high school yearbook: girl most likely to go to Hollywood.

She walked the ten blocks to the Monroe Institute, a modern five-story building with rows of impact-resistant windows overlooking a large parking lot. The floors numbered from one to five indicated the level of severity of the illness, with the administrative office being on the first floor. Renata chuckled at that. The ward and the interview rooms had been on the third floor, so she asked at the nursing station and was told Dr. Enright was probably on a coffee break. She followed the corridor to the B wing cafeteria.

"Do you remember me?"

Dr. Enright frowned, pretending he could not place her. "You work in the kitchen, I think." He stirred his coffee. "Now I remember. You're one of the cleaning staff. "

"You still like to play games."

"With you, Renata, it's all games."

"I don't usually come in here to this particular restaurant, but I had the strangest urge for a coffee, at this particular restaurant, strangest thing, and then oh my gosh, I saw you sitting here, and oh my gosh, what a coincidence."

"What a coincidence. Strangest thing. Sit down. I'll buy you the coffee you had the strangest urge for."

She pulled out a chair. "I came to thank you, Dr. Enright. As the result of your help I have not murdered hardly anyone since I last saw you, so the time I spent in your storage room was not wasted. Don't think of yourself as a diagnostical failure. We had a lot of good conversations."

"Yes, we did."

"I'm a hairdresser. I listen to people all day long telling me their stories. I watch their face in the mirrors. I have two walls of my salon lined with mirrors. From watching from several directions at the same time, I've learned to read people. You were easy to read, Doctor, easy to play games with. I read many things about you, but the one important thing I read was that you are a doctor who wants to help people, not a doctor who wants to click checkboxes in a pizza place."

"I won't be blackmailed into seeing your sister, Renata."

"And I won't blackmail you, Dr. Enright. In fact, I'm starting to believe that, after giving it some thought, some of what you got me to tell you might even be true."

"Well, it's up to you to figure out what's true and what isn't."

Renata glanced at the tables next to them, an assortment of unkempt patients sitting with a mish-mash of visitors and staff, all dressed in drab uniforms. Although Renata had the picture she wanted to show Dr. Enright in her hand, she could see in Dr. Enright's eyes what he was looking at: a flower in a weed patch, today her blonde hair pulled back in a ponytail, her blue eyes highlighted with blue eye shadow and the bruise on her cheek there, but not too obvious. She gave him her best coy smile, a tilt of her head, telepathically saying, You've never met anyone like me before, have you, Dr. Enright? The chemistry was there, she could feel it. She said, "I know you've been thinking about me, and I've been thinking about you."

"What have you been thinking?"

Renata stared at the doctor with what she knew was her most worshipful demeanour. "When I first saw you, I thought you looked too young to be a doctor. You're probably older than you look. You look sort of like Brad Pitt; you know, he still looks about forty , but I think he's over fifty."

"Well, thank you. I take compliments whenever I can get them, even when I know they're being given by someone with an agenda. You're a charmer, Renata. You could sell a camera to a blind man."

She said, "Well, I'm not here to sell you a camera, but I am here to show you a picture. Just before they let me go, I went to arts and crafts. The teacher bounced and smiled. She was young, probably a student, full of energy and cuteness. I wanted to say no, arts and crafts is not my jar of jam, but I figured not participating would be considered "uncooperative," which would mean no privileges. So I followed the group shuffling along the hall to the arts and craft room, which was at the opposite end of the hall from the lounge and the cafeteria: ten little tables with coloured paper, brushes, watercolour paint, easels. No one was particularly interested in spite of the energy of the teacher, but they drew and dabbed and painted.

"I wasn't planning to draw anything. But I had to do something. So, I sat at the table. I'm not much of an artist but I began to draw, letting my pencil go where it wanted. First came the outline of a sock with the two knitting needles crossed at the top, then, as I filled in the details of the sock, which should've been some kind of pattern, I saw that I was drawing a girl."

She handed him the picture. "I have no idea how I managed to draw that. I'm no artist, that's for sure. It was like someone else took the pencil and drew it. It was spooky, Dr. Enright, like an unseen hand dropped that pencil on my paper, a woman's hand, the hand of a women, I swear, Dr. Enright, the hand as it drew the lines rattled clickety-clack like knitting needles, clickety-clack. It was freaky. It was like those fingers were Nana's fingers, drawing herself."

Dr. Enright studied the picture before handing it back. "Very clever. From our conversations about the knitter knitting the knitted, you've turned the knitting needles into a tree, so your next line will be something about being the fruit of the poisoned tree."

She took back the picture. "Which picture of Renata do you now have in your head, Dr. Enright: this picture of me you tried to create for your police assessment, yes the fruit of the poisoned tree, or the picture of me I created for you to take home with you at night, or the picture of me you are right now seeing across from you in this cafeteria?"

When Renata reached up and undid her ponytail and shook her hair down around her shoulders, she knew that his eyes had been opened and when those opened eyes slid from hers to the bruise beneath, she knew that he had chosen the right picture.

Renata reached up to touch the spot. "My father. Comrade Ivan. But the bruise will be gone in a day or two, and so will Katria if I don't get her into a hospital."

"Does he hit Katria, too?"

"Yeah, he does, that's for sure."

His right hand that had just picked up the cup set it down. He leaned closer. She was sure he wanted to touch the bruise, run the tips of his fingers along her cheekbone. When she bent over to tuck the tree picture away in her purse, she let her hair fall forward, leaving it there for a moment before sweeping it out of the way. "I'm due for a perm, I think. Give it a bit of a curl. I hate giving perms and I hate getting perms. Oh god, another perm. Men's cuts are the best. Quick and easy, in and out."

Dr. Enright smoothed down his hair, which was parted on one side as usual. "I'm never happy with the cut I get. I'm sort of fussy. It's always too short. I end up shorn. I say just half an inch, but half an inch usually ends up one inch. Don't they teach you about rulers and measurement in hairdressing school?"

She leaned forward to examine the cut. She reached out to touch but then stopped herself. "Do you mind? I can tell by the feel. I think it wasn't layered properly."

She ran her fingers through his hair, just a little above the ear. "I can fix that. It just needs to be layered a little better. I've been doing more razor cuts to give my fingers a rest. Not many do it anymore. If you come by my salon, I can do it for you. A good cut will make you look like a good doctor, the same as a good perm will make me look like a good hairdresser."

He hesitated. He said, "I hate to be vain, but I do like a good cut. Whereabouts is your salon?"

CHAPTER TWENTY-EIGHT

Dr. Enright arrived at The Cutting Corner right on time. Before entering the shop, he glanced in the window. When Renata saw him, she smiled her perfect smile and waved him in. Her casual ponytail, black sweater, and blue jeans, stylishly tight, patched, and faded, drew him back to all the beautiful university girls he'd missed out on because he was always studying. He followed the swing of her hips to the chair at the back of the shop. He glanced at her in the mirror as she slipped on the cover.

The fact was, haircuts made him apprehensive, too short at the back, too short on top, the soup bowl, a tuft sticking up at the crown. When he asked for the back to be made longer, the rest ended up too long. But he began to relax, confident that this girl would do it right. She gave that impression: smart, decisive, and competent. Too competent. No airhead hairdresser, this one. So be careful, he warned himself as he settled into the chair. She has an agenda.

She arranged the sheet around him. As she fastened the back, her fingers brushed along the nape of his neck, then strayed over to the lobe of his right ear, up along his temple, and back along his neck. He was not in his office now and she was not a patient, so he settled himself into the spell of her stroking fingers. And, as she moved around to the front and leaned a little forward, the low-cut sweater six inches from his face caught the attention of his involuntary biological imperative. Of course, he told himself, that's why some women dress as they do. Not all, mind you, like that weather girl who accused the news station of sexual harassment for making her stand sideways while doing the forecast. Renata would be more than happy to stand sideways to do the weather.

In the mirror, standing sideways, she caught him staring. He lowered his eyes. She picked up her spray bottle. She began, her left hand running again along the back of his neck as she sprayed. She caught him looking again, so, embarrassed, he focused on the rope-pattern stitching on the pockets of her low-slung jeans. The gold-studded leather belt served no purpose except decoration; her jeans were too tight to need holding up. She'd need help getting them off, maybe. To move his thoughts in a different direction he shifted his focus to the rise of his Oxfords sticking straight up under the sheet.

"You're not going to go bald," she said. "By your age, if the hair is going to thin, it will have already started. How old are you? Well, if you don't mind me asking."

"Thirty-seven." Not Dr. Bornstein yet. Still time to make up for lost time, he thought, as he watched her hips shift a little to the side to examine his crown.

Her hand lingering along his neck, she said, "From the conversations you and I had, I now understand Katria's problem. What she needs more than anything is someone who will explain to her why she's reacting the way she is."

"It's me you're talking to, Renata. I'm a paying customer here for a haircut. Forget the con."

"Is it okay if I do a razor cut?"

"Of course."

"About Katria…"

"I know all about Katria. I'm here for a haircut."

But then, with the glint of the razor flashing from the overhead light as she raised her arm to make her first cut, a vision of himself carrying home his head under his arm jarred him to attention: which Renata at this moment was she?

He held up his hand to stop her. He tried to make a joke of it. "The Barber of Seville. Does this chair lean back into a trap door, slit the throat, tip back the chair, and down I go?"

"Relax, Dr. Enright. Why would I kill the one I have chosen to cure my little sister?"

She set to work, razor and comb slicing with remarkable speed along his left side, so quickly he feared for his ear. He remained rigid in his chair, afraid any movement might jar her arm.

But she continued to talk as she sliced. "Just … you know … in my business, I listen to everyone's story; everyone has a friend or a brother with some kind of mental disorder that keeps them drugged up like zombies. That is, if they even have a doctor. If they don't, there's a two-year waiting list to get one. In two years, Katria will be long gone."

If she was concentrating on talking, she was not concentrating on the razor that was now shearing the hair off the right side of his head. "Renata, please. Put down that razor."

She stopped, the razor and comb suspended mid-air. He pushed back against the seat, waiting for her to switch hands so she could sidestep into the slice that would cut his neck in half. He almost shouted, "Why don't we make an appointment right now for her to see me in my office?"

"Oh my gosh! Dr. Enright!" She beamed at him, her smoke-blue eyes watering up with what looked like genuine tears. "I could hug you right here on the couch. I know she'll like you. You're young and cute and if you relax for five more minutes you'll have a haircut like Brad Pitt and I'm sure she'll have a crush on you the minute she sees you."

He glanced from the razor to the door, uncertain whether to leap out of the chair and run or stay put and save his dignity. He tried to get up but she put her hand on his shoulder. "Dr. Enright, I'm almost finished."

He tried to settle back in his chair and relax. Finally, when she set aside the razor and continued with scissors and comb, he breathed a sigh and settled into watching her thinning scissor movements in the mirror. When she set her tools aside to finish off with the blower, his attention wandered to the perfect fit of the tight jeans and sweater over every curve, no slack in the arms, no bulge across the tummy. How could such a beautiful young woman be anything but beautiful, inside and out?

She placed her hand on his shoulder and turned the chair this way and that so he could see in a hand mirror the size of a tennis racket the back of his head, and also, in the opposite larger mirror, the half-moons rising under the scoop-neck sweater.

"Perfect." He managed a smile at the best, absolutely the best haircut ever.

As he climbed out of his chair, what caught his attention in the mirror was the swing of the hand that had held the razor reach up to the bruise under her eye. She turned his way so he could have a better look.

He said, "I've been thinking..." He considered each word, fearing he was moving in a direction he shouldn't go but needing to regain his dignity. "I have to get going. But as a doctor I can't let that bruise go."

She raised the hand to touch the bruise. "I'm sure it will be gone in a day or two. But not the haircut." She fluffed it up. She said, "That's part of the problem. You're drying out your hair too much and splitting the ends. You shouldn't use high heat. You shouldn't use a drier at all. And don't wash your hair with hot water."

He followed the swing of her hips past the three chairs to the back of the shop. He gave her his card. She bent over the machine to run the card, unfolding her arms a little to allow her left shoulder to open the view in the mirrors so sparkling clean that there was no way his eyes could escape the reflection.

"Uhhh ... I've been thinking..."

She gave back his card.

"Uhhh ... Renata. Step over here by the window."

In the natural light, he could tell the bruise was not recent, any remaining swelling now covered with makeup. She stood before him, her face tilted up. "I should be at a meeting," he said. "But that can be skipped. Can Katria meet us here?"

She stepped back. "That's not possible. I can't spring it on her. She'll refuse to come. Two weeks ago, her aunt Gizla died. Two days ago, they found her nana dead on the storage room floor, heart attack, same thing."

Dr. Enright felt alarm in his voice. "Another heart attack?"

She turned away and began to tidy the shelves under the mirror. Finally, he managed to ask the question: "Did they do an autopsy?"

Renata wiped at her tears. "She was a hundred and two years old. Ivan had her cremated. Said it was cheaper."

Renata began to slowly fold the cover. "I've got an idea." She wiped a tear from her cheek. "Why not come over for dinner Sunday night at my place? I'm usually home by about six, so any time after that, say seven. I can tell Katria you're dropping over as a friend, sort of, and yes he's a doctor, but he's lots of fun and he's cool…" Renata hesitated. "I'm being too pushy … just a thought…"

Dr. Enright knew he was being manipulated in a direction he didn't want to go. He knew he should say no. But what about another heart attack in the family? On the storage room floor, no less.

Maybe Nana's death was a lie to trick him into seeing Katria. All manipulators are liars. Well, we're all born liars. He said, "Not dinner, Renata. A twenty-minute meeting with Katria. If I think she needs to be hospitalized as a danger to herself and in danger from her father, I will phone the ambulance and have her committed."

CHAPTER TWENTY-NINE

Dr. Enright checked his watch: six fifty, right on time. He had intentionally not dressed casually. A suit and tie for a professional visit. He parked half a block down from Renata's low-rise red brick building on Sherbourne St., walked back to the entrance, and opened the door into a small lobby. Against one wall was a series of 1960s mailboxes with call buttons. He pressed the button for R. Boscov and her cheery voice said, "Come up, number five."

There was no elevator, so he climbed the open stairway to the second floor. To his left were numbers two and three, so he turned right, walked to the end of the hall, and tapped on number five. She opened the door immediately. She was dressed in black tights and a loose, checkered shirt. Her blonde hair was tied in a ponytail and, without makeup, she could have passed for a teenager.

He stepped into a large living area with conservatively matching blue sofa and chairs, teak end tables, a blue curtain over a large window. Everything neat and tidy, even the desk in one corner of the living room: four pencils in a round holder, sharpened, point up.

"Lovely apartment, Renata. I'm impressed."

"What were you expecting?"

"I think a little more … I don't know … hippie. This is tidy and organized."

"You should know the diagnosis for tidy and organized, Doctor. I was praised by my father for being neat and tidy, so when I want to feel praised, I go tidy. Usually, the place is a mess. It's the parent over your shoulder thing. Would you like a drink, Doctor?"

"No thank you, Renata. This is a professional visit, to talk to Katria."

He sat on the edge of the chesterfield, his back straight, ready to excuse himself and leave if Renata started any games. She was dressed conservatively enough but the hair pulled back in the ponytail reminded him that at the appropriate moment, she'd undo it and shake it out and release the temptress, at which point, he had promised himself, he'd walk away.

She disappeared into the kitchen and returned in a few minutes with two glasses.

She said, "Vodka and lemon. A drink always makes you feel better."

"I won't be manipulated, Renata." He set the drink on the end table. "Is Katria here?"

"Not yet. But she will be."

"If Katria isn't here, what's the point?"

"She's coming. Let's have a drink. A sure cure for everything. Sure beats pills. Good for what wails on you."

"Wails on you?"

"Like in your asylum, wailing."

He sighed. Katria probably wouldn't show.

"Dr. Enright. Relax." She sat beside him on her edge of the chesterfield. "She's coming. She might be on her way right now." Renata handed him his drink, half a tumbler of vodka with a slice of lemon.

He waved it away. "How about you phone Emma and see if she is on the way."

"All right, Dr. Enright. In a minute."

When Renata settled into the soft cushions, Dr. Enright's mind flipped back to Renata on the chair in his office, her bathrobe half off, her PJs undone. He crowded himself against the armrest.

"I know what you're thinking, but for goodness' sake, Dr. Enright. Undo your tie, sit back, and relax. I did my best to get her here but with mental patients, things don't always work out exactly the way we intend. So have a drink."

He was not separated from her by his office desk. He was in her territory, in her living room, seated on her couch. She was sitting next to him. He checked his watch and made a mental note. Five more minutes.

"The vodka is a Russian thing. My grandfather taught my father and he taught me. Now I kind of enjoy the ritual. You mix the vodka, slice of lemon, stir it once with the finger, and down the hatch."

"Ivan taught you? How much does he drink?"

"Like a fish. He comes home after a hard day spent poisoning God's little creatures and knocks back three vodkas."

"I've never been a drinker. What is special about vodka?"

"In the war it was cheaper than water. One thing my nana — God rest her soul — taught me is that nothing should go to waste. She'd buy a chicken at the market, and we'd eat the chicken and then she'd make soup out of its feet. She'd put the pot on the table with the feet floating on the top, looking like the chicken had come back to life and was upside down in the pot. No eat, a good swat, into the storage room you go. From the war. Nana hid out in a basement storage room during the war and ate chicken feet. Rats too, probably."

Dr. Enright leaned back in the chesterfield. Everything either made sense or didn't, depending on the context.

"You have to let the vodka sit a minute for it to get absorbed into the lemon. Wodka, my nana called it. May she rest in peace. Then you put in your finger, not so much to stir it, but to force the juice out of the lemon. It looks like a stir but it isn't. The finger goes once around with the lemon against the glass, and then down the hatch."

"Lemon included?"

"Not included. That's why you drink it down in one drink, so your top lip isn't tripping over the lemon. Watch how I do it."

Renata stirred the drink, swept the glass up to her mouth, and tilted her chin. Down the hatch.

"Like that." She settled back into her side of the chesterfield. "I bet you can't do it."

He picked up the drink and smelled it.

"Don't be a sissy."

He stirred it. He examined his wet finger.

"You can lick it if you want afterward. First, you drink."

He took a tentative sip.

"Nana would drink her drink and lick her finger and then ten minutes later she'd say, 'Don't lick your finger, Dearie.' She always called me Dearie. After her third wodka she'd turn kind of dazed like there was a gas leak, and she'd say, 'Find my program on the television for me, Dearie.'"

He took another sip.

"I'll show you. You have to cock your finger." She grasped his hand and cocked his finger to one side and held the glass to his lips. Afraid he'd spill down the front of his shirt, he gulped down most of it, but the glass was not high enough or the hand was not quick enough, so the lemon got in the way.

"Try again," she said, "You're not cocking your finger. Take off your tie first so it doesn't get spilled on and then cock your finger."

He took off his tie. He finished the drink without spilling but then almost choked on the lemon which he spit out into his hand. With the back of one finger he wiped away the drops of vodka hanging from his nose.

"Renata. This is embarrassing."

"Now you lick your finger, not that finger, the other finger … unless you want me to lick it for you. But you have to cock it first."

He licked his cocked finger.

She mixed two more. "You almost got it, but you're not doing it fast enough. You've got to pin down the lemon, pin that sucker down, and then quick, down the hatch."

This time he concentrated on squashing down the lemon and then quickly down the hatch. But lemon included. He spat it out.

"I know. You're using the wrong finger. You've got to use this finger." She held hers up. "This pinky is the one you use. Try one more."

For this one, the third, he squished down the lemon, curled back the finger, and quickly down the hatch, no lemon.

"Perfect," she squealed. "Now you've got it. Now you lick your finger."

He licked his finger.

"One more time," she said. She took his glass for the fourth refill. "I want to see you do it in one shot, pin the sucker down and down the hatch."

He hesitated.

She stared at him, waiting. Then, before she could say 'don't be a sissy,' he did it, perfectly. He settled back on the couch, proud of himself.

"You forgot to lick your cocked finger."

He licked his cocked finger.

"That's not right. Do you want me to show you?"

"Renata."

"Yes, Dr. Enright?"

"How can there be a wrong or a right way to lick your finger?"

"You don't lick it like you're a kid licking the chocolate cake icing, like ten licks. You put it right in your mouth. Here, give me your finger."

She took his finger and put it into her mouth, all the way in, ran her tongue around it, and gave it back to him. "Like that. So you're not wasting any. That's what it's about. Think Russia in the war, not wasting any."

Dr. Enright was feeling a little dazed, like there was a gas leak. Already he had almost forgotten that he was there in a professional capacity. Although now that he was there, now that he was sure Katria was not coming, since he was there anyway...

"While you're waiting for Katria, I know she's on the way, would you like a quick something, like potato salad with ham and green beans? Better than a cafeteria sandwich in the nuthouse with the wailers and the wilters."

"Wilters?"

"You should spend more time in the ward, Doctor. The ones that look like they've had an electroconvulsive accident."

"Oh."

"I'll have to cook the potatoes. It won't take long. I'll put on some music."

Dr. Enright was feeling warm in his suit jacket. It was not a hot day and not particularly warm in the apartment, but he was feeling clammy. He removed his jacket and folded it over the back of the chesterfield.

But now he was sitting in his shirt, minus his tie and his jacket. Before he could move to an opposite chair, she returned from the kitchen. She sat down, still on her side, with two fresh drinks.

"Willie Nelson," he said, noticing the music she had chosen.

"Oh my gosh. You know Willie Nelson. I thought you'd just know the classic guys. Like that Fingero guy."

"I think it was Figaro."

"Fingero. One two three, we do it together." She put the fresh glass in his hands. She shifted his suit jacket to sit closer. They each inserted the finger, stirred once around the glass, and lifted the drink in unison. This time he managed it perfectly.

"Perfect. You're going to make a good Russian. Here, give me your fingero." She took the extended finger and inserted it into her mouth and massaged it with her tongue.

"Now you do my fingero."

She inserted her finger into his mouth and he massaged it briefly and she withdrew her finger.

He set down his glass. "I think we're getting a bit off track, Renata. The reasons I came … The reason I came, Renata. Tell me about Katria. No, better still. Tell me about Katria's Russian family back in the war. That is where everything starts."

"Back in the war. Well, my father's father beat him, our father beat our mother. Did you know abused children make good soldiers? It gives them a chance to be the abuser. Anyway, I hid in my bedroom and listened to him say his after-words: 'sorry, sorry, never again.' I heard them a thousand times, first the poisonous words and then the antidote words. How does that work, Dr. Enright? Are both words coming from the same person or is the same person really two different persons? I knew that's what you were trying to make me into in your assessment, two different persons, the abused becomes the abuser, so I knew from experience what sort of mental case fuckery was going on. And then my mother would say, 'I think he needs someone else; I think he needs someone better; I'm not good enough for him.' How does that work, Dr. Enright, that his words become her words so now she is two different people, the beaten blaming herself for creating the beater."

Renata turned a little on the couch. She brought one leg up underneath her and faced him. "We're all just people pretending that no kind of fuckery is happening until, too late, there's the result of the fuckery. Her name is Katria."

Dr. Enright picked up his suit jacket. "This isn't right, Renata. Katria is not here and I'm leaving."

She shifted her butt so that she was closer. "Did you like licking my finger, Dr. Enright?" Renata reached up and undid her hair and shook it down over her shoulders. She smiled, barely, the corners of her lips upturned just a little. "Shaking my hair down, what I did just now … it feels good to open the storage room door to let myself out. It feels like putting on a black dress with a cinched waist. I have one. Do you want me to show you?"

Dr. Enright knew that now was the time to get up and say goodbye. But then, when she said, "Maybe not. Maybe you should go," he felt liked he'd been shoved out the door, like it was her decision, not his.

But then, when she said, "But let's finish our drinks first," he felt like Renata had cancelled her decision to shove him out the door so now he could make his own decision.

She downed her glass and he downed his glass. When she held out her finger, he sucked it. When he held out his finger, she sucked it. She reached over to stroke along the hairline at the back of the neck. "The cut is good, I think." She touched the tip of his ear. "Just a shade below the ear." Her hand strayed down along his arm and returned to her lap.

She picked up his jacket, but instead of giving it to him, she folded it over the opposite chair. She sat closer to him. She ran her fingers through his hair just above his ear. The fingers strayed down to brush across his earlobe. "I'd like to see it a little longer at the side, like in the old Robert Redford movies. Not now, he's too old, but the younger Robert Redford. Rover Redford, I called him, because of all the women he seduced."

She shifted closer, leaned back, and gently began to touch the skin under her eye with the fingers of her left hand while the fingers of her right hand began to play with the top button of her blouse. Slowly and methodically, she unbuttoned the second button, and then the third button. She picked up his hand and slipped it into the neck of her blouse to the back of her neck.

She said, "This is where it hurts. Right here. Well, sort of. Just an ache along this side. From when he smacked me."

Like an arrow through a Valentine's Day heart, Dr. Enright came to attention. He was a doctor. An involuntary doctor-response sent his hand further into her blouse to run the tips of his fingers along her collarbone. "Any pain here?" he asked.

"No. It's the back of my neck."

His fingers explored along her neck and shoulder and back along the collarbone. She turned her head to allow him more access. She pulled her blouse aside. He felt along her neckline to the back of her neck, pressing gently in random locations. As he moved closer and raised his other hand to draw her closer, the fifth Russian Valentine arrow hit him.

"Would you like another Russian, Dr. Enright?"

Because they were sitting so close, this was a whisper in his ear, a warm breath along his neck that shifted his body a little closer for a closer examination. But before he could respond, she put her hand on his arm. "The potatoes. I'll fix you another Russian while I do the potatoes."

"I can book you in for X-rays." He tried to straighten up and put himself together. He had never booked anyone for X-rays. He was a psychiatrist.

"I'm sure I'll be all right. I'm sure I'll recover."

He watched her do up the third button of the blouse. He watched her do up the second button of her blouse. He attempted to sit upright but seemed unable to move, trapped in fact.

She went into the kitchen. He thought he should call a cab. But he did not stand up and get his phone from his jacket pocket. He closed his eyes and drifted. He listened to the refrigerator door open and close, open and close. He heard the clink of glasses, tinkle-tinkle, as she brought in the drinks.

He pulled himself upright.

Renata handed him his glass. "I've heard that shrinks becomes shrinks for the same reason priests become priests. Hiding from their demons, or in the case of shrinks, trying to shrink their demons. What exactly are you hiding from? Spirits? Demons? Urges. I think urges. You said I was screwed up from childhood stuff. How about for you? Tell me. Lie down here on the couch and tell me."

Dr. Enright lay on the couch. Renata pulled up a chair beside him. "Close your eyes and tell me about Dr. Enright the little boy. Imagine yourself as a little boy. It's called role-playing."

"I hid my toys under my bed, under the mattress."

"Well, this is no good. If we're going to role-play, we have to be in the bed, not on the couch…"

"I might be drunk but I'm not…"

"Yes, you are drunk. Get up." She helped him up and led him to the bedroom. "Get under the covers." She pulled them back and pushed him down and covered him up.

"Close your eyes. It all starts in childhood, Dr. Enright. You have to go back to the child to understand your problem. Close your eyes and imagine."

He closed his eyes.

"Are you imagining?"

"I'm falling asleep."

"Well, wake up. Pretend I'm your mother tucking you in." She picked up his arms and situated them under the sheet and smoothed down the covers. "Did your mother give you a goodnight kiss?"

"Yes, always."

She put her lips over his and flicked her tongue into his waiting mouth and then, coming down beside him, whispered in his ear, "You're a little boy now. You've had tuck-in and good-night kiss … now what? What comes to mind?"

"My train set."

"Tell me about your train set."

"It was a train set."

"Imagine yourself as the little boy when you tell me about the train set."

"I had a wailway twack and a choo-choo twain."

Renata sat up. "That you hid under the covers?"

"Under the bed."

She settled down beside him. She nuzzled his ear. "So … tell Mommy … why do you hide your wailway twack and choo-choo twain under the bed?"

"I don't hide it there. I keep it there."

"Why not in your toy box?"

"I like to lie in bed and imagine I'm the twainman."

"Do you blow a whistle?"

"I do, yes."

"And do you shoot off a little steam?"

"Yes, I think I do."

"How old are you now, when you're playing trainman and blowing your whistle and shooting off steam into your toy box with your mother. How old are you."

"About five, I think."

"I think you need to tell Mommy more about blowing your whistle and shooting off steam."

"What's there to tell?"

"Let's go back to tuck-in and good-night kiss. Show me how your mother does the good-night kiss."

Renata leaned over and put her mouth over his and ran the tip of her tongue over his tongue. She sat up. "You did that with your mother? You were five years old lying in bed blowing your whistle and shooting off your steam into your mother's toy box. Is that what you're telling me?"

"Renata."

"Yes, Dr. Enright?"

"Why do you always twist everything around to make it sexual?"

"You were the one blowing your whistle and shooting off your steam while you kissed your mother. What was she wearing while you were kissing?"

"Usually her PJs and bathrobe."

"Ahh. Now we're getting somewhere."

"Renata, I think we're both drunk."

"Show me how you blow your whistle. Let me see you do it."

"I can't."

"Of course you can't. You can't blow your own whistle. That's your problem. That's where your feelings of urges come from. From not being able to blow your own whistle."

"I did blow my whistle. I pulled, you know, the rope. And I let off the steam."

"Ahhh, now we're getting somewhere. When you pull the rope out comes the steam. Show me your rope."

"Well, I don't have it here."

"I bet you do, Dr. Enright. You can't fool Dr. Renata. Let me see you pull your rope. Here, I'll help you." Renata reached down to the waistband of his trousers. "Just relax, Dr. Enright. I know it's hard … oh my gosh is it hard … but you have to learn to relax. Sometimes people aren't sure what's troubling them. They just know something isn't right. And in your case, do you know what isn't right, Dr. Enright?"

"What isn't right, Dr. Renata?"

"I know what you think I'm going to say, but you're wrong. You had no ticket to insert into the ticket thing. You had a choo-choo and whistle and a rope and the steam and just a minute—" Renata let go of the rope and sat up. "That's why you wanted to believe I had jumped in front of the subway train. It wasn't the subway train, it was your choo-choo train, because the minute you saw me you wanted to grab hold of your rope and blow your whistle, from wanting to do what, Dr. Enright. Say it out loud."

"Say what out loud?"

"When your mother gave you a goodnight kiss, what did you want to do? Insert your ticket. Do you understand, Dr. Enright? You took away my clothes, dressed me in PJs and a bathrobe like your mother, then you turned my subway train into your choo-choo train so you could act out your desire to insert your ticket. And then what did you do? You manipulated me into inviting you here so you could insert your ticket in my bedroom. All because you had a mother who dressed herself in PJs and a bathrobe and teased you with kisses but never let you insert your ticket."

Renata slid her hand down his side and fastened it around the rope again.

"I think this is very serious, Dr. Enright. You're going to need a lot of therapy, otherwise known as mind-fuckery. And now that I've got you in my assessment room, you will be staying here until I decide you can go. You know, Dr. Enright, I'd have gladly pretended to be your mother and let you insert your ticket. And I'd have pulled your rope, too, if only you had asked, and let off the steam right there that first day in the hospital. Just pull that rope and insert the ticket and blow off the steam and everyone is happy and I go home and don't miss two days' work. Instead, the minute you saw me still fried from my birthday, you already had your plan baked into my birthday cake."

"Renata?"

"Would you like to insert your ticket or do you want me to keep on pulling your rope?"

"Inserting your ticket and pulling the rope is not the same as hiding away my toy choo-choo."

"No, it's not, just as clicking your mouse on a page full of mind-fuckery checkboxes is not the same as — oh my gosh, Dr. Enright. Let me write this down like a trauma narrative: Dr. Enright came into my bedroom. He was breathing heavily and when he climbed into my bed, I saw that he had hold of his ten-incher, hard as a rock, wanting me to wrap my lips around it and wrap my tongue around it. He was breathing so heavily I thought Miss Fiddle across the hall would hear. I wanted to tell him to keep quiet but I was enjoying his moans of pleasure and enjoying my sucks on it like a ten-inch lollipop. Oh my gosh, Dr. Enright. Let go of me so I can grab my bedside diary and my freshly sharpened pencil. September 24. Dear Diary. Dr. Enright, my love. My fingers tracing your sweet lips and your moans of pleasure as our tongues search for one another. That look on your face, Dr. Enright, breathing hard as you run your hands over my amazing body, the bed almost too small for your enormous dick. That look on your face, Dr. Enright, breathing hard, your head falling back, oh my gosh, lustus eruptus."

When Dr. Enright finally managed to open his eyes, she showed him what she had written. "Am I being blackmailed, Renata?"

"Well, it takes two to wiggle. And you should have known better. You should have known the moment I let down my hair I would have you in my snare. And you shouldn't have dressed me up in pyjamas and a bathrobe and locked me in your storage room. Not my jar of jam. That pissed me off."

CHAPTER THIRTY

At four o'clock on Sunday afternoon she set off by subway. She didn't need to worry that on this day Comrade Ivan might have changed his mind and decided to do something besides shredding his Mastercard statements into a steady whir, like, say, killing something. Comrade Ivan had himself on rigid schedules that he couldn't break, even if he was the one who put himself on the schedule in the first place.

The day she had done Aunt Gizla, the jar was one-third full. The afternoon she did Nana, the jar was only one-quarter full. She had used two teaspoons each on Aunt Gizla and Nana. How many would the comrade need?

She found him sitting at the kitchen table sorting through his bills, receipts, and papers, unlike Nana who would have been watching her Sunday afternoon TV movies. The last time she'd been to see Ivan, he'd been watching a movie, but not a Hallmark like Nana. In this movie, the boss and his secretary were doing it on the floor of the boss's office.

He glanced at her. "That get-up you're wearing is disgusting. Have you no shame?"

She sat opposite him at the table.

"If you're going to dress like that, leave."

He continued to whirr through his Mastercard receipts.

She raised her voice over the hum of the machine. "Before I slam the storage room door on you for good, before I shut down the Big Shredder, no more shredding me into ribbons, I'm here to give you a chance to apologize."

He continued to shred.

"How much do you weigh, if you don't mind me asking?"

"None of your business."

"Probably about 180."

She had guessed Nana was 150, but Nana was fat; Ivan was all muscles. She'd need at least four teaspoons. If she gave him too little, he wouldn't die; if she gave him too much, it might be traced. Two for Nana, maybe three for Ivan.

She stretched her feet out in front of her and slid down on her spine and waited. Then she asked, "Aren't you going to tell me to sit up straight?"

"Sit whatever way you want. It's your spine."

"An appropriate movie for you to be watching right now would be a murder mystery. I learned from watching the undead movies that homicidal ideation is better than suicidal ideation. In homicide, the one who dies is the one who deserves to die — well, depending on your point of view."

He continued to shred.

"I heard on the news that the dog poisoner was using ten-eighty. So I thought, what better way to get the poison out of my heart and into the poisoner's heart? It even sounds poetic. And better still, as I watched Nana and Aunt Gizla having their heart failures, I could see in real time my heart failures that had been going in slow motion, one slammed storage room door at a time. Know what I'm saying?"

"I haven't got a clue what you're saying."

"I didn't believe you could be the dog poisoner. But then you poisoned Algernon. And I want that glass thing back."

"What glass thing? What are you talking about?"

"On the shelf. What I gave Moms for Christmas. If she tipped it up it snowed on the snowman. After the snow cleared a little sign next to the snowman said Merry Christmas. When you gave it to her you said, 'Now you can say Merry Christmas to yourself.'"

"Bring me a Russian."

"Good idea. Drink a glass of spirits because pretty soon you'll be a spirit, know what I'm saying?"

She went into the kitchen. She scooped out one teaspoonful from the mustard jar and poured it into the glass. Then she put the pickle on a little plate just the way he liked it and then she stirred in two more teaspoons for good measure.

She handed him the glass and sat down. He stirred it with his finger and brought the glass to his mouth and drank it down. She settled herself into a chair. He set down the glass.

"Do you want another?"

"If I have to listen to your drivel, I might as well have a Russian while I'm doing it."

She got up and took the glass out to the kitchen and came back with a refill, a little more poison added, thinking the first must be working through the bloodstream, already racing through his veins to his heart.

She handed him the drink and sat down opposite him.

He held up the glass, sighted through the drink, stirred it with his finger, and gulped it down. He took a bite of the pickle and continued to shred. Why is it taking so long, she wondered. By now, his stomach ought to be cramping, his breathing going shallow, his throat gurgling. Why is it taking so long? By now his brain should be turning into a paste.

Suddenly his face drained pale, as though his heart had stopped pumping. He seemed to be looking off somewhere, maybe at his regrets. He reached up to slap at the air, as though the maggots from Mom's coffin had flown over to show him the way to the cemetery.

Now he was doubled over in his chair. Now his breath rattled in his lungs as he clutched at his stomach. But she did not get him up out of his chair to put him in a storage room, because Comrade Ivan had never put her in a storage room. She left him in his chair. As soon as he'd stopped jerking around, she took off his shoes and socks and started with the big toe of the right foot. But not in proper order starting with one and ending at ten but, to annoy him, painting this toe here on this foot and then one over here, at random, like Moms would do. Either way, Moms would say, what's the difference? You still end up with ten black toenails.

Then she took his knitting needles from the kitchen drawer and bent them crooked. Then she wiped away her prints. Then she dialed 911. Then she hurried out the door and along to the corner. Then she waited for the sirens and the blinking lights. Then they pulled up to the front of the house. One paramedic, a woman, got out of the ambulance and stood on the front lawn. She seemed to be double-checking the house number. Ivan's not going to like her standing on his grass, now walking across the lawn and up to the door. His last dying breath will be spent asking her doesn't she know better than to walk on the lawn. The paramedics wheeled in the gurney, then returned in a few minutes with the body. Ha. Let me get the door for you.

CHAPTER THIRTY-ONE

In Dr. Enright's office in the Monroe Institute, dressed in a heavy blue coat, baggy jeans, and baggy T-shirt, in the chair opposite his desk, his nemesis sat. With sunken, listless eyes, she stared at her feet, not looking at him.

They looked alike, obviously sisters, but Katria was no Renata and he knew immediately that for the length of the interview, Katria would be sullen, withdrawn, and non-communicative.

"Ready to get started?" he asked.

She didn't look up at him.

"Would you like to take off your coat?"

"No."

Not unusual: the coat, for a teenager, was often, in a threatening situation, a security blanket.

Dr. Enright opened the top drawer of his desk. He handed her a picture of a man standing at a window staring out. Inside the man's chest was a vulture with piercing eyes pecking at his heart, stripping it away one piece at a time. Underneath it said: Write down the name of the vulture and the name of the person. He handed her a pen. She studied the picture, then she curled her free hand around the writing hand. Then she gave the picture back.

He said, "You have named your aunt, your nana, and your father as the vulture, and yourself as the person."

She shrugged.

He handed her a picture of a person with a hole in the chest. "After the vulture has consumed the heart, what's left?"

She shrugged.

"Guess."

"The empty body?"

"I think so. Yes. The empty body remains but the vulture has spread its wings and flown off. With the heart. Who is this person?"

"Me."

"So who has won?"

She looked up at him. "The vulture?"

He handed her a third picture. In this one, the person was at the window with heart intact and the vulture was off in a tree. "Who is the person?"

She rounded her shoulders and huddled under her coat, emotionally curled up in her head. She stared at her shoes and then, with the toe of one, she slipped off the other to reveal her naked foot with black nail polish.

Dr. Enright said, "Katria. Help me find your heart."

She looked up, straight at him. "Why did they become vultures?"

"I don't know, Katria. I would like to ask you that question."

She slipped off her other shoe.

"I sucked my thumb. So Nana glued my thumb to my finger with crazy glue."

"What?!"

Startled, Katria looked up.

Dr. Enright said, "Sorry. I shouldn't be surprised. Go ahead."

"First, she showed me a picture of a guy hanging upside down from his feet that were glued to the ceiling, and then she glued my thumb to my finger."

"In other words, she threatened to glue you upside down to the ceiling? Did you report that?"

"I told my father. He said 'A lot of things around here need gluing.'"

"Why didn't you tell your counselor at school?"

Katria shrugged. She stared at her naked feet.

"Why? Give it a shot."

"Whatever I told the counselor, my father would deny."

Dr. Enright wrote it down. "All right. Let's make some sense out of this. Why did they not want you to suck your thumb?"

"They said it would give me buck teeth."

"So there's some logic in there. Logic mixed up with crazy."

"When he took my mother to the dentist, Comrade Ivan — that's what we call my father — said to fill the cavities but don't use freezing. She's sneaking donuts. Otherwise, she wouldn't have cavities."

Dr. Enright wrote it down and frowned. "I'm surprised the dentist didn't give her freezing anyway."

"He refused to do her teeth if he couldn't give freezing. He said he wouldn't charge. But Moms thought she deserved it because she ate too many donuts."

"Ah, yes. Of course. The perfect victim. For the abuser, a match made in hell."

Dr. Enright showed her a picture of the person with a heart, no vulture anywhere. He laid it beside the other three pictures. "Which picture should you start looking at?"

Katria shifted her feet. When she reached down and pretended to take off her socks and put them in her pocket, Dr Enright stood and leaned over.

"Why did you take off your socks when you weren't wearing socks?"

She jammed her socks further into her pocket.

He said, "Your traumatic childhood memories are like an invisible vulture pecking at your heart. You need to get them out where you can see them and look at them and then get rid of them. And I know you know that because I just watched you take off your socks and try to get rid of them."

Her eyes came up to his. She reminded him of one of the two girls who came into the coffee shop he sometimes stopped at, about twelve years old, very quiet and mousy looking, not one of the popular kids, but he could tell they were inseparable. They weren't alone, no matter how terrible their parents were, these two girls had one another.

Tears began to trickle down her cheeks. Katria stared at her bare feet.

"I noticed you've painted your toenails black."

She nodded.

"Why are you staring at your shoes?"

"I'm staring at my socks."

"Your socks are in your pocket."

"No. They're still on my feet. I can't get them off."

"Ah ... Brilliant." Dr. Enright wrote it down.

She glanced at him, waiting for his next question, but instead, he set his pad aside and leaned back in his chair. "Everyone has a knitter, Katria, and everyone is knit, one stitch at a time. If you were knit by your parents, you'll be the same as your parents or the opposite. Either the same sock or the opposite sock. But either way, you're knit to be what they made you. A sock can't be something other than a sock. If it tries to become something else, like a scarf, it has to unravel itself, which is what you've been doing and why you're here talking with me. But now it's time to reknit yourself."

Silence.

Dr. Enright watched her withdraw into herself and pause for a moment's self- reflection as she considered what he said.

"Our hearts speak to us, but not always in words. What is your heart telling you?"

She shrugged.

"Katria. Your mind is telling you lies. But your heart is telling the truth. The rattle of those knitting needles in your mind will turn you into a skeleton of dry, lifeless bones with black toenails if your heart doesn't get help."

Dr. Enright glanced at his watch. His time with Katria was up. He had a meeting to attend. But he needed to get an answer to the question he had been asking himself since he met Renata.

He asked the question. "Which Boscov is evening the score?"

He watched her slip her feet back into her shoes. She got up and closed the door and was gone.

Several weeks earlier, Dr. Enright had chaired a session of the Gatekeeper Program, designed to alert front-line subway staffers to watch for possible jumpers, individuals who loitered on the platform, many of them teenagers. He had learned that, for some unknown reason, they would take off their shoes before they jumped, hence the name the media had given the phenomenon: Empty Shoe Suicides.

Dr. Enright stared at his notes. Without intending to start a file, he had started a file. Dr. Enright picked up the phone and dialled the number of The Cutting Corner. When Renata picked up, he asked the question, "How did Katria get here and how will she get home?"

"By subway," said Renata. Then she added, "Ivan has had a heart attack. He's in a coma."

Dr. Enright hung up.

CHAPTER THIRTY-TWO

Katria had been in the Bloor-Yonge subway station hundreds of times, but never until this day had she seen the sign on the subway wall: "Thinking of Suicide? Call 142. Let's talk." The arrow pointed to a phone beneath the sign.

What would they do if she dialed the number? Stop the train just in time? What if she didn't dial the number? Stop the train too late? Send her father a bill for cleaning her up off the tracks? Ha! She liked that idea.

She stood by the newspaper box and waited for the train.

What would the driver think? A driver like her father would say, The stupid kid jumped in front of the train. A driver like Moms would curl up on the couch and not talk to anyone for days, maybe go jump off the subway platform herself. A driver like Renata would go to a bar and drink Russians. A driver like Emma would sit down and bawl her eyes out.

Katria had taken off her watch and set it to an incorrect time of ten-twenty, her third-last act of defiance. Comrade Ivan always needed the clocks set to the exact correct time; like a cuckoo bird, every two days he checked his clocks. Her appointment with Dr. Enright had been at two o'clock, so by now it must be about three o'clock. There were not many people on the platform to look down and say, She was so young, her life had just started, why would she do such a thing?

She was thinking, I'll pretend I'm Algernon and climb down off the platform and into the tunnel where no one can see me, in the maze with walls on all sides looping around and back to the beginning. Algernon could follow his tracks, so he'd know after one time around that all the tunnels looped back to the beginning. They were dark but that would not bother Algernon. He followed his nose, which was smarter than Katria's brain. She'd get lost in five minutes and Algernon would win. But still, providing she followed the train tracks, she'd eventually loop back to the beginning, round and round until the train came.

Katria sat beside the newspaper box to wait for the train. The headlines in the newspaper box said, "Brampton Mayor Has Stroke but Lives." They showed a picture of him in his hospital bed, flowers at his bedside. She read the write-up: the stroke that went right through his brain had turned him into a Charlie, dumber than a mouse.

Katria remembered Emma had brought Algernon flowers from the store. She'd set them up on the dresser and arranged them nicely, but she didn't tidy up Katria's things like Ivan did. She left Katria's things the way they were, clothes all over the place, and books and homework, all of it a big mess, but then right in the middle, an arrangement of flowers. Algernon liked that.

Katria should've written Emma a card saying she was sorry, explaining it wasn't Emma's fault, she had done all she could. She'd have written it like Charlie, with all the words spelled wrong. She'd discovered the book *Flowers for Algernon* after she had gotten her essay back and the English teacher had corrected her spelling. She'd been afraid to take it home, so rip, tear, gone into the library garbage. She checked the book out and showed it to Renata, who said Ivan did the same to her with the spelling. "So," Renata said, "I spelled everything wrong on purpose." The next day, Renata had brought home a white mouse for Katria, who named him Algernon. That was around the time Renata had stopped cutting Ivan's hair because she was having trouble resisting the urge to slit his throat with a razor. Then Emma bought Katria a copy to read to Algernon.

Katria wished she had long legs like Renata. Katria wished she had a hospital bed like this man in the newspaper who'd had a stroke. And was paralyzed, it said. But they were going to do therapy to see if they could get his brain to work a little better. So that instead of being dumber than a mouse he'd be smarter than a mouse, and might even be able to spell right.

She could feel the platform shake and she could hear the screech of the iron wheels on the rails. She took off her shoes. She laid them down side by side, left-right. Then she turned one backward, her second-last act of defiance.

CHAPTER THIRTY-THREE

The nearest subway was Bloor-Yonge, a five-minute walk — or a two-minute run. Dr. Enright descended the subway stairs two at a time and emerged onto the platform. There were no gawkers, no awestruck bystanders peering down onto the tracks or into the tunnel, which meant no "unsafe platform" condition had been issued by the TTC.

He found her huddled in one corner of the concrete wall, hiding under her coat, her shoes lying beside the newspaper box. Dr. Enright sat beside her. When he reached out to take her hand, which was stuffed in the pocket of her jacket, she looked at him, startled. Her eyes were empty: no sadness, no anger, nothing.

He said, "The coat is covering the body, Katria, but it doesn't cover the hand. Give me your hand."

She gave him her left hand. He took it in his right and covered it with his left.

"Hands, Katria, are like feet. There's a left and a right. But unlike feet, hands are magical. They're capable of knitting, yes. But they're also capable of leading. And of helping. And of holding. And of protecting. I know you can't believe in words, but maybe you can begin to believe in hands."

From the tunnel he heard the screech of the subway train. It rattled up to the platform and stopped. They waited for the passengers to get off and get on. They waited for the tunnel to swallow the rumble and rattle of the subway.

"Think of the knitter, Katria. The knitter takes fine virgin wool, pure and untouched, and works it into narrow bands of one particular colour, carefully stitched and pressed and woven. But sometimes, so preoccupied with the knitting is the knitter that the knitter fails to see what her hands are knitting."

Katria said, "I don't think you know how to knit, Dr. Enright."

Dr. Enright let go of her left hand and with the tip of his finger wiped away the tears which were welling up into Katria's eyes. When he put his arm around her, he could feel the bones of her shoulder blades shivering through her heavy jacket.

They waited.

New faces emerging onto the platform cast casual glances his way, a man in a suit comforting a teenage girl, probably father and daughter.

Dr. Enright waited, either for the next train so that he could accompany her home and leave her to whatever fate she might create for herself, which from now on as he lay awake at night would be like waiting for the predator vulture of guilt to start pecking at his mind, like waiting for the telephone to ring and on the other end hearing Renata say, You managed to make time to spend three hours getting drunk with me, but all you could give Katria was an hour, with no repeats.

Now under his arm, he felt her body relax as she settled herself against him. She lifted her hand from his and used it to wipe at her tears. Dr. Enright reached over with his free hand and picked up her empty shoes. He slipped the left one on her left foot and the right on her right. The imaginary socks he took from her pocket and threw out onto the far side of the subway tracks where she could see them. They waited for the next train. The train rumbled out of the tunnel and into the station. After it had gone, they saw that the clickety-clack of the wheels had so torn the socks to pieces that they were gone. He held out his hand for her and together, hand in hand, they left the subway platform.

. . .

"We have no beds, Dr. Enright. Where are we going to put her?"

"Put a gurney in one of those assessment rooms. And get her on an IV. Even if she wants to eat real food she probably can't. And get her on one-to-one monitoring her food intake. She's top priority."

Dr. Enright went down the hall to his office and phoned Renata. " I've had her committed. She can't leave until I say so."

CHAPTER THIRTY-FOUR

The nurse waited while Katria took off her street clothes and put on hospital PJs and a housecoat. She lay on the gurney. The door swung open and a second nurse appeared. She wheeled the IV into the room and attached the bag.

"I need your arm, Katria. This won't hurt. Just a little prick."

She poked in the needle and taped it down and got it started.

The nurse sat down on the gurney. "I'm Miss Finn. Might as well get to know one another while we're waiting."

"Waiting for what?"

"I can't leave until the IV is finished."

"Why?"

"Because you'll pull it out."

"Oh," said Katria.

"I saw you when they brought you in," Miss Finn continued. "Do you remember? I looked at you and you looked at me."

"No."

"Do you want to hear what Dr. Enright said?"

"What?"

"Like empty shoes, she walks without a heart."

"Oh."

"Do you know what I saw? I saw a teenage girl with a child's eyes. I've worked before with binge dieters, revenge eaters. Diet fanatics. Everything about the body is shrinking, but not the eyes. The eyes get so big and so empty and so desperately hungry. That's what those eyes say to me, loaves of bread everywhere but not a slice in sight. The mind can lie to the body but it cannot lie to the heart, and the heart cannot lie to the eyes."

They watched the IV drain into her arm.

CHAPTER THIRTY-FIVE

Renata took the empty elevator of the Monroe Institute and got off at the fourth floor and followed the arrow pointing to reception to the right, next to an open door with a sign for offices.

"Katria Boscov," she said to the receptionist.

The lady typed in the name. "What's your relation?"

"Sister."

The lady searched Renata's face. "I need ID."

The lady phoned the ward to say Katria's sister was coming. The elevator to the fifth floor worked on a buzz-in system. The doors rolled open and she was met by a nurse who led her to the lounge where Katria, in hospital issue PJs and bathrobe, sat on a faded green chesterfield next to a patient with the same wilted, musty look as the other patients. Katria seemed thinner than Renata remembered, her hair stringier, her face paler.

"So how do you like it here?" asked Renata, sitting in a blotched sofa chair which at one time must have matched the chesterfield.

Katria didn't look at her.

"Your room okay?"

"Everything included, one low price."

"Including drugs," said a wire-thin girl in the next chair. Her face was scabbed, like an addict. "In the morning your meds, then seven o'clock breakfast in the caf. Then eight o'clock room tidy and laundry and write your goals, ten o'clock snack. They got this trolley deal that comes up on the elevator, then noon meds and one o'clock rec room, you play cards and stuff, then two o'clock group and then meds and then meds and then meds. They don't allow mental patients to get better; otherwise, they wouldn't sell any meds. So they give the pills out in pairs: number two cancels number one, number four cancels number three…"

Renata took Katria's hand. "The nurse told me you had a room now. Let's go to your room so we can talk."

Katria got up and led the way across the lounge to a room three doors down from the nursing station. They sat side by side on the bed, Katria leaning forward, elbows on her knees, staring at the floor. Her face was empty, no expression, no one home.

"What kind of drugs?"

"Antidepressants, I guess."

Renata remembered a patient on her ward who could rattle off his meds — oxycodone, Valium, Thorazine, temazepam — but could not remember his name or walk a straight line.

Katria said, "Did someone bend Comrade Ivan's knitting needles straight again, because I can hear them clickety-clack, all day long in my head."

At first Renata thought she had not heard the question properly. "Ivan didn't knit. He just liked to arrange them, you know, make geometrical patterns."

"I know. Now they're too crooked to make geometrical patterns."

Renata's first thought was, how could Katria know about Ivan's knitting needles? Renata searched her face, trying to find Katria. "Have you got something to tell me?"

"About what?"

Her expression remained blank, a zombie stare. She lay back on her bed and closed her eyes.

Renata decided that Katria was too stoned to know what she was saying. So Renata said, "My next visit I'm going to bring my kit, you know, the one I use when I go to the retirement home. I'll do your hair."

"Bring money for the vending machine."

Renata got up and left the room. She counted seven patients in the lounge, sitting around the television, bodies with brains that couldn't be fixed, two of them skinny as skeletons. She walked across the lounge to the elevator and pressed the button. When nothing happened, she pressed it again.

"You need a key," said one of the skinny ones. "I'll get the nurse."

When the nurse arrived, she inserted the key into the button lock, and the down arrow lit up. Renata stepped in and pressed the button. She returned to The Cutting Corner to get ready for the next day: first customer, Mrs. Rawlins.

CHAPTER THIRTY-SIX

First thing in the morning, after a breakfast of one poached egg on toast, Katria was taken to the ward and introduced to Elaine, who was sitting next to a short girl called Jennifer with eyes like aimless marbles.

"This is how we sit," said Elaine. "You got Cindy's room so you get Cindy's chair. They moved her to the Electric House to rewire her fuses. That's where lifers go, like Dominic the rocker, over there, rocking his breakfast. That's where he's going. He's already been four times."

Dominic sat rocking on the floor in the corner. With fleshy jowls and a slice of belly hanging over his belt, he looked like a heart attack commercial.

"He killed his own family, so he's a lifer."

Katria looked around, but Moms wasn't there. "He killed his family? Now he's here for life?"

"Don't give Dominic your pills," said Jennifer. "He hides them in a jar underneath his bed. Every day he takes them out to examine them and count them. He says when he gets a hundred, he'll take them all. But they're all crumbling and coming to pieces because he handles them so much. Nobody wants to steal them because they're full of germs. He doesn't even wash his hands after the bathroom. Pretty soon, he'll have handled them into powder and he'll have to snort them."

...

Katria lay on her bed and listened for the tap of Renata's six-inch heels bringing the news: Comrade Ivan had a heart attack. Renata would sit down on the bed, no makeup except eyeliner, and cross her legs in her designer jeans. She didn't need makeup, her skin was perfect like her body, no snacks at the cart for Renata.

From her chair in the lounge, Katria watched both Emma and Renata step off the elevator, right on time for two o'clock visiting hours, Renata flouncing in like Scarlett Johansson. Renata motioned for Emma and Katria to follow her along the corridor to Katria's room. She climbed up on her bed and Renata settled down in the chair while Emma stood by the door.

"When is the funeral?" asked Katria.

Emma came over and sat next to Katria. "Nana's funeral was nice. Mostly people from her church. They said nice things, said what nice person she was."

"Who was?"

"Nana."

"Nana, a nice person?"

"That's what you do at funerals. Say how nice the person was."

"Tell lies, in other words."

"Tell lies, yes," said Renata. "That's why they have flowers at funerals. It's from the old days, when they believed the smell came from the lies everyone was telling."

"I meant when is Ivan's funeral."

"He didn't die, Katria. He's in a coma."

Katria's heart skipped a beat. She looked around but Moms wasn't there. For a moment, her thoughts went blank. But then Katria had a lightbulb moment, like that guy who noticed the apple fall to the ground instead of staying up in the tree. He saw the apple and said, Just a minute, how did the apple that was up there end up down here?

"So ... you mean ... his body is still alive but his brain is dead, not alive?" Katria couldn't believe it. A Zombieland dream come true.

Moms had turned Comrade Ivan into an undead dead, complete with black toenails. Ha! Katria pictured him lurching up the graveyard lane, meeting Moms face to face, well look who's here, Dr. Boscov. Ha! You're looking a little undead. You seem a little off tilt. Here, let me help you with the door.

Renata pulled out the little haircut suitcase that she used when they called her into the old folks' home, all leather with the combs and the scissors and the brushes. Katria sat in her chair. Renata snapped open the cover. Katria watched Renata remove the scissors and the comb. Renata fastened the sheet under her chin. She began to fuss with Katria's hair.

Renata said, "The doctor likes it curly. While you're sitting there talking to him, tilt your head a little to the side and run your fingers through your hair."

Emma scowled. "Don't tell her that. That's called flirting."

"That's called getting away with it. That's what this is about. Fire is the devil's only friend. What have you got to tell us, Katria?"

"Nothing."

While Renata finished wrapping the first ribbon of Katria's hair and started on the second, Katria couldn't stop thinking, Wow! Ivan is with the Walking Undead.

When they were done, off Emma and Renata went, down the hall, Renata with a flounce and a wiggle, like Scarlett Johansson wearing Paris Hilton's designer jeans. Not even Comrade Ivan, who used to take the flounce out of everything he touched, had been able to take the flounce out of Renata, nor had he been able to take the flounce out of Katria. But ha! She had taken the flounce out of him.

...

Katria lined up with the others at the meal trolley, brought up from A-wing in the basement. They had a butcher down there who cut the cow front to back, starting with pot roast Monday, Tuesday ribs and Wednesday steak, and then Thursday stew, and Friday, Saturday, and

Sunday, meatloaf from all the stuff left over on the floor. Monday, he started on a new cow. The kitchen lady wheeled the trolley into the small dining room set up for twelve plates, twelve patients.

"You're looking a lot better, Katria." Miss Finn said the same thing to each patient every day, even to Dominic. "Put these on, Dominic. You can't walk around in bare feet."

Miss Finn walked with Dominic from the trolley to the table and waited while he put on the slippers.

Miss Finn walked over to get Jennifer who had taken her plate filled with food and stood at the window looking through the wire mesh. "You're looking a lot better today, Jennifer. Take your plate over to the table and try not to eat anyone else's today."

CHAPTER THIRTY-SEVEN

Dr. Simpson was in the cafeteria having lunch with a nurse. He noticed a young blonde girl in tight jeans and a sweater come into the cafeteria, hesitate for a moment looking for a table, then come directly his way. She sat at a table next to his. When he stood to leave, she approached. "Could I have just one quick word with you, Doctor, about private convalescent care? The hospital phoned about it, for Ivan Boscov. I'm his daughter."

"Renata, yes. I got your message." He extended his hand. "Ivan is doing better than expected. He's a fighter. He'll soon be able to go home."

The nurse slid back her chair and excused herself, saying, "See you at one."

Renata considered the vacated chair but did not sit down. "That's the problem. He should go into convalescent care."

Dr. Simpson sighed. "If only." He shoved his empty lunch plate aside. "But there are no beds. Oxford would be the place for Ivan, but it's full. No beds anywhere, for that matter. He'll be an outpatient discharged to you or Emma with visiting nursing care."

"Ivan is abusive."

"Abusive? Well, he won't be now. He's paralyzed down one side." He glanced at his watch and then at Renata: an extremely attractive young lady, he noted. Also, he noted, a very worried young lady. "I've got a few minutes. Let's talk about that. Sit down, please."

Renata eased herself down in one gracefully fluid motion onto the chair, and there she was, sitting across from him. Her blue eyes, accentuated with blue eye shadow, caught his and lingered.

Dr. Simpson worked long hours. The nurses were out of bounds as far as hospital administration was concerned. He had considered dating sites, had even googled a few. But he always avoided blondes because he'd read that they got twice as many hits as dark-haired girls. And dating took time, with all the preliminary getting-to-know-you stuff. So he was always on the lookout for one to drop out of the sky so he wouldn't need to spend time looking.

Here she sat and, he realized, noticing her sidelong glances, she seemed especially interested in him.

"I was suspicious," said Dr. Simpson. "I ran some tests. Confidential at this point. But in the message, you said he poisoned himself? Why would he do that?"

"Easily answered. Ivan worked in the rodent control business. He used an extremely lethal poison imported from Russia called ten-eighty. Ivan is Russian. In Russia, they have a tradition: they stir their vodka with their finger, they lick the finger and they drink the drink. Ivan was a heavy drinker, and he was not careful about washing his hands after handling the ten-eighty, so he was probably mixing the poison into his drink. Probably not immediately lethal, but over a long period of time, yes, of course lethal. He's probably had trace amounts of poison in his blood for years that finally caught up with him."

Dr. Simpson liked this girl; not only was she attractive, she was articulate. "Well, Mr. Boscov was conscious for a few minutes yesterday, not aware enough to say anything. But heart attack victims do recover, and when they do it takes a day or so for their thoughts to get working. So no point in going further on this for now. When Mr. Boscov recovers, he'll give us the answer."

Renata settled herself on the chair, trying to get more comfortable, it seemed. As she leaned forward and crossed her legs, he noticed a bluish tinge like a bruise on one cheek. An eye shadow smudge, he concluded.

"Surely there must be space for him somewhere," continued Renata. "It doesn't have to be in the city."

Dr. Simpson checked his watch. "Would you like a cup of coffee, Renata? I still have a few minutes."

"That would be lovely."

But then, checking the cafeteria lineup, he said, "Probably not. Not enough time."

"Coffee's not good for you anyway." She smiled a row of perfect teeth.

"But tell me, Renata, how are you doing? Two funerals, I understand, and now your father. Unfortunate, yes, more than unfortunate. As I said, I think it's suspicious. Although, as you said, he handles poison. Maybe that's what happened. It's like how we draw relationships with carpenters and pressure-treated wood and lung cancer. They breathe in wood particles, the same as asbestos workers breathed in airborne asbestos."

"So that is your conclusion?"

"No, it isn't. Trace elements might have caused renal damage but not heart failure. But I don't know. When Ivan comes out of his coma, we can ask him a few questions. And we're still doing tests."

"Well, whatever," said Renata. "We're still left with the problem. Emma can't look after him. She's got a business to run. I have a small apartment. Even with visiting care, it won't work." She ran her fingers along the bluish shadow. "Bruises heal, but the abuse doesn't."

He scowled at the bruise, nothing more now than a faint discolouration. "When did that happen?"

"The day before his heart attack. Nothing serious, one of his standard backhands."

"Private care, then. Can you afford that?"

"Well, I'm only a hairdresser. Not rich, that's for sure. And Emma is up to her eyes in debt."

"A hairdresser. Yes. Emma mentioned that. Whereabouts is your salon?"

"On Church Street, not too far from here."

"Do you do men? I never get the cut I want."

She examined his cut. She reached up to turn his head a little but stopped herself. "Sorry." Her hand fell to her side "How do you like it?"

"Left long, usually."

"How about a sampler haircut. If you don't like it, you don't pay. The Cutting Corner."

Dr. Simpson checked his watch. "Hmm. Maybe. I might be able to work that in. The Cutting Corner." Dr. Simpson stood and extended his hand. Her fingers were long and slender and her eyes, smoke blue, were magical. And that smile. "I'm in the OR in ten minutes, but later today I'll phone for an appointment."

CHAPTER THIRTY-EIGHT

Katria was still in bed, barely awake, at six-thirty in the morning — and there was Elaine, sitting almost on top of her, asking, "So how is your day going so far?"

Katria blinked her into focus.

"I bet they're going to send you to the Electric House. It's like a separate building behind the Cathedral. Dominic wasted his family so they sent him to the Electric House. When he came back, he could pick up cellphone transmissions. So they sent him down again. This time he came back with a tin foil hat. When he put it on…"

Katria sat up and rubbed her eyes. "I know. He could get Netflix."

"No, he could talk to dead people."

"Dominic is crazy."

"This is the crazy house. If you're at the dance, you act like you're dancing. If you're at the skating rink, you act like you're…"

"Skating. I got it." Katria wrapped her bathrobe around herself and followed Elaine to a chair in the lounge. Dominic came shuffling over, his eyes staring down at the floor and his arms hanging loosely.

"It comes to him by ESP. You can watch him when it happens, certain times of the day you can sit in the lounge and be real still and watch. He pulls out his pad and pencil and writes but not really because it's the dead person that writes for him. That's why, when you ask him, he says he doesn't remember writing it. In the Electric House they made his brain cells magnetic. He acts dumber than a bowl of salad but that's an act. What really happens, you watch him, he feels a buzz, you watch him, he feels a buzz in his fuses and his eyes light up in neon, picking up dead people's thoughts like telepathic information. Hey Dominic. This is Katria. Give her a message from ... Who do you want a message from?"

"I can already talk to my mother. How about ask my dad, ask him if he's dead yet."

Dominic's nose twitched. He leaned his head to one side, listening, nodding, trying to lick up the spit forming on his lower lip and running down his chin and through the black stubble of his two-day beard and under his double chin to soak into his shirt collar.

Dominic pulled out a little notepad and began.

Elaine explained. "Sometimes he writes like in poems or sometimes like in billboards with pictures or sometimes the dead people use him to post complaints about whatever bugs your ass when you're dead."

For five minutes, Dominic's fingers spun back and forth. He handed Katria the notepad. He had drawn a picture of Ivan dressed in the same suit he had worn on his first date with Moms. Next to it he'd drawn a picture of Ivan laid out on a table in the undertakers. Next picture was Ivan lying in a coffin, still wearing the wedding suit, but he was missing his socks and his toenails were black. Next was a picture of Ivan's wedding suit in his coffin, all piled in such a heap that you'd need a stick to sort through the mess without touching anything if you wanted to find what was left of him.

"Cool," said Katria.

...

Katria lay on her bed, drifting on her meds. She imagined she was lounging on the beach. She imagined she heard the phone ring. Moms said, Wake up, Katria. Some bad news...

The head nurse, leaning one shoulder against the door frame, one foot over the other, said, "Wake up, Katria. Some good news. Your father is a fighter."

"Fighter? Who did he fight?"

"No, he's a fighter. Like you."

"Someone punched him out? He's dead, I hope."

"Well, he should have died. But he's a fighter like you. He's being discharged in a few days with visiting home care. He's a fighter."

"Shut up about the fighter. He had a heart attack. You mean he didn't die yet, like he's still not dead?"

"He's paralyzed on one side. But the speech will come back. Usually, with a heart attack or a stroke, speech goes into park for a while, but it will come back, bit by bit. For my mother, it took six months. But she was old. Your dad, he's a fighter."

CHAPTER THIRTY-NINE

Emma sat in the only chair in Katria's hospital bedroom and waited. The bathroom door opened and there Katria stood in hospital PJs and robe. After an awkward silence, Emma said, "So now can we talk?"

Katria shrugged. She climbed onto the bed and propped herself up with a pillow and stared out the window.

Emma waited.

Finally, Katria said, "The nurse asked me if I wanted to send my dad a sympathy card. I said I would rather send sympathy cards to the owners of the dogs he poisoned."

"Do you have anything to tell me, Katria?"

Emma waited. Through the open door, she could see the nurses crossing back and forth on silent shoes from one room to the next, monitoring wherever needed. Emma came over and sat on the bed and put her hand on Katria's arm. She said, "Now they're talking about three heart attacks in a row and Ivan being poisoned. If we're lucky, he'll die before he names who did it. But what if he gets his speech back? Then what?"

Emma climbed up on the bed and put her arm around Katria's shoulder. "Dogs look up to people as though they aren't crazy. Cats look down at people as though they are crazy. I think we should be looking at people with the eyes of the cat to figure out what to do next."

Emma waited. Finally, she said, "You're not crazy. Ivan is crazy. But what if he wakes up, crazy or not? Are you in trouble?"

Katria tucked her legs up tight underneath her. She said, "I used to wish I had a guard dog who would bite them every time they picked on me. But I knew if I got a dog, they'd drive the dog crazy. They'd like, step on the dog's toe and the dog would yelp and they'd do it again and the dog would go into the corner out of the way and so it would go until the dog would turn and bite and then they'd say, the dog bit me, the dog must be punished. Put it in the storage room."

Katria got up and went to the window. From the window, without turning around, she said, "Across the street from Moms's cemetery is a little park, nice and green with a big tree. It's there right now. It doesn't go away. I look out the hospital window and I can see it even though it's ten blocks away. An old man comes three or four times a day with his dog, not a little yappy dog, a sort of sheepdog. The man carries the leash in his hand and the dog carries the stick in his mouth. For about half an hour they play fetch, that little dog never once drops the stick. Then the dog carries the stick back home and the old man carries the leash back home. So I started to wonder what will happen to the dog when the old man dies and instead of being over there in the park he is over there in the cemetery. So one day, one Saturday, I went over to the old man and said, 'If your dog ever needs a good home, here's a number.' 'Well,' he said, 'as a matter a fact, I have to go into a retirement place. I can't keep my meds straight. I've been asking around to see who would take him.' So I said, 'When do you go into the home?' 'End of the summer,' he said. 'I'll fix it,' I said. So I gave the old man Renata's number at The Cutting Corner. I said, 'Tell Renata the story. She's very smart. She can fix anything.'"

"And what can Renata do to fix what you've done?"

"Watching the dog fetch the stick, like in my mind going to the same place, again and again, bringing back the same stick, so many sticks to fetch. The stick was crooked, but all the time the dog was carrying it, it was straight."

"So what can Renata do to make this straight?"

Katria came back and sat on the bed. She said, "I talked to one of those talking turnips at school counselling about Algernon. He looked at me with those jury's eyes and didn't say anything. So then I told him about the stick man and his dog that Renata would fix. So the talking turnip asked me why don't I replace the mouse with the dog so I said yeah but my father wouldn't allow the dog to carry a crooked stick."

"Katria. Look at me. Who killed Aunt Gizla and Nana?"

She shrugged. "I don't know. Ask Dr. Goldstein. Aunt Gizla and Nana each had a Dr. Goldstein. He saw everything with big eyes that never blinked. I think that's why they didn't beat me even though they probably wanted to."

CHAPTER FORTY

The worms and maggots are missing out on their coffin creams because Comrade Ivan is undead when he should be dead. So why don't you take a wander over, Katria, and help him along. But remember, he'll want a proper funeral with the proper format: Number one, drain the blood; number two, pack the butthole with cotton; number three, lay him out in his coffin; number four, the people come in and out to have a look; number five, six feet under, starting to rot, the worms and maggots already enjoying their coffin creams.

Katria watched the nurse use her key to call the elevator. She stepped in and pressed the button and the doors rolled shut, leaving Katria to watch the numbers flash down: 3, 2, 1, and stop. Then they flashed down to B. Then they started up again: 1, 2, 3, and the elevator doors rolled open. The lady from the church auxiliary stepped off the elevator, pulling her snack cart behind her.

Katria went over to her chair and sat down. She tried to put together a plan. She watched everyone line up for cookie time. First, the dribblers and the shufflers from B wing. They had names but no one knew them. They were allowed street clothes but never bothered to wear them. Then the lifers who wore street clothes and never changed them. They spent their days dreaming up new symptoms so they wouldn't get discharged.

"I want a chocolate chip," said Hopscotch Ralf to the auxiliary lady, who had big white hair and a body shaped like an ice cream cone. Hopscotch thought she was the Good Humour ice cream truck woman.

"We don't have any chocolate chip ice cream, but how about a chocolate chip cookie?"

Today Hopscotch was wearing his hospital robe and, hopefully for the auxiliary lady's sake, his PJs.

"But oh my, aren't you looking fine today, Ralf. And such a lovely day. It's sunny and warm and clear. And today is Tuesday. Only twelve days left in October."

She said this every day to Hopscotch, hoping to sidetrack his mind from what it was planning: to give her a hug and a lick.

"Chocolate chip," said Hopscotch, opening his bathrobe and — oh my god — reaching out his arms.

The Woman's Auxiliary lady backed away to the other side of her wagon and pretended she didn't notice as the nurse stepped in and led Hopscotch away, leaving the lady standing at her cart, probably trying to think of a nice comment which would make Hopscotch think she hadn't turned him down, rejected him, because after being licked by Hopscotch she'd never feel clean again. But rule number one: You must never reject the patients, even the ones with black teeth, and especially Hopscotch, who spent each day hopscotching imaginary squares, waiting for her to arrive. All he wanted was a hug and a lick and maybe a little extra and there he came again, Here I am, here I am, breaking away from the nurse, straight at the ice cream lady, waving at her, the nurse chasing along behind.

This is no place to be if you're looking for a girlfriend, Hopscotch.

The auxiliary lady straightened up the cart and put the lid on the cookie tin and fastened down the milk jug and started off toward the elevator.

"Way to go, Hopscotch," said Elaine. "Ruin it for everybody."

"Ralf can have a cookie instead." The nurse took Hopscotch by the arm and led him to the wagon and he helped himself to a cookie. "I'll look after Ralf. Everyone else line up for a snack."

So the auxiliary lady started again, opening up the wagon and taking the lid off the milk jug and giving out the cookies. After everyone was finished and she had tidied her cart, she used her special key to call the elevator. She got on the elevator. The doors rolled shut.

That key on the little hook on the auxiliary cart, said Moms. If you could get that key. Sometimes if the elevator is too busy, the lady's auxiliary comes up the stairs with the help of two of the men from the kitchen. If she loses her key, which she often does, she calls down to the kitchen or asks a nurse to open the elevator.

...

"My, aren't you looking fine today, Ralf. And such a lovely day. It's sunny and warm and clear. And today is Wednesday. Only eleven days left in October. Wouldn't you like to have a glass of milk and a cookie?"

They had turned up Hopscotch's meds, but that didn't always work.

Moms said, They should glue his left and right forefingers together so he can feed himself but not open his arms enough to try for a hug.

Katria said, But that wouldn't work. When he opened his arms just a little bit, his bathrobe would fall open, peekaboo, no bottoms.

Still smiling, no nurse in sight, the auxiliary lady backed away to her wagon and pretended she didn't see. She straightened up the cart and took the lid off the cookie tin and opened the case of individual milks. As Hopscotch hopped up for his hug and his lick, bathrobe hanging open, the auxiliary lady distracted, Katria slipped into her pocket the key hanging from the handle of the cart. Katria knew the auxiliary lady would look for the key and, oh my gosh, she must have left it in the kitchen so the nurse would call the elevator and if they couldn't find the key in the kitchen someone would give her another key. The kitchen was about cooking a cow not about getting a lick.

Moms said, During seven o'clock TV time, while the nurses sit at the station writing stuff down for the shift change, we call the elevator, slip out the front door, take the subway to Toronto General and be back before the nurse does the lights-out ride at ten o'clock. Even if we aren't back, it won't matter because as long as our light is out, they don't go into a dark room.

CHAPTER FORTY-ONE

Emma arrived at Renata's door in a state of panicked confusion. "I was getting dinner ready when the phone rang. Ivan will be discharged to me in a wheelchair. He's paralyzed along one side, can't talk, but in a week or so they're sending him home. I tried to explain that I don't really live here but it didn't matter. I'm his daughter living with him in his house; he'll be discharged to me. What am I going to do?"

Renata led the way into her living room and sat on the chesterfield. Emma disappeared into the kitchen. Renata heard the muffled rattle of the refrigerator door opening and closing and the clink of the glass as Emma mixed two drinks.

"This vodka," Emma said. "You got me started, now look at me, an alcoholic, like Ivan. Every time I mix one, I remember him saying, Don't use ice cubes. So I'd put the ice cubes back into the tray and then Ivan would say, don't put them back in the tray. You've already handled them. You put in new water. So I'd say, so what. They're frozen."

Renata sat next to Emma. "Now he's frozen."

"I wish. He's up walking, sort of. Like lurching. But yeah, walking."

They did it together, stirred with the finger and down the hatch, no spills. "Perfect," said Renata. "There must be some word you say in Russian when you drink, like gesundheit."

"I think that's for when you sneeze. And that's not Russian."

"I was thinking, Emma. Say you and Katria move in with me. There'd be no room for Ivan and his wheelchair so he'd have to stay in his own house with homecare. We stage it for when the worker comes, like in real estate, make the home look homey, except the opposite. Move some of your stuff in here to make it look smaller. And, guess what: there's no wheelchair access. When the social worker gets here to check it out, you leave that part up to me."

...

Renata answered the knock and the Home Health Services worker stepped in right on time, two o'clock. She was a middle-aged woman in a blue business suit and black loafers. Her briefcase and her scowl suggested a no-nonsense investigator.

Renata had left clothes all over the floor and sour milk on the kitchen table along with plates smeared with catsup and three condoms on the floor beside the unmade bed.

"They can't keep him there much longer," Carla repeated. "Once we teach him the exercises, the rest is up to him."

"But there's no wheelchair access."

Renata watched Carla clear a place at the kitchen table and open her briefcase to take out a file. She didn't seem to care about wheelchair access or about the mess or about the hopelessly crowded apartment.

"But if he gets out," Renata argued, "and has another stroke. Then what?"

"You call the ambulance."

Emma appeared in the doorway. Renata had dressed her in a miniskirt and low-cut blouse and made her up like a street worker.

"Emma has met someone." said Renata. "Her new boyfriend is moving in. "

Carla gave Emma a judgmental scowl. "Your husband is one week in the hospital and you have a boyfriend? Does he know about this?"

Renata picked up on the "husband" error. "That's the problem. If he comes home and finds his wife … When he finds out about it…"

"Maybe he's already guessed," suggested Carla, looking around. "Maybe he already knows."

"Guessed, but not knows. When he gets out, he'll find out for sure his wife is unfaithful and then who knows what will happen. She's already told him she doesn't love him anymore. She's already told him she wants a divorce."

"Well, now you have a reason to get back together. You're going to have to try to make things work."

"She doesn't want to go back with Ivan. She wants to stay with her new boyfriend. She wants to marry him. She wants to be with him forever. She wants to have his children. Ivan belongs in a home and the government should provide twenty-four-hour nursing care."

"It's too unsettling for me," said Emma. "I just got out of rehab for my vodka addiction…"

"I know it sounds cruel, Carla." Renata put her hand up to rub her forehead. "The whole business is giving me migraines. We are trying to find an answer."

Renata turned to Emma. "Let's consider this. He's in a wheelchair, he's not going to know where you are, you can meet Boris in a motel every afternoon, that sort of thing. And that other guy you've been hanging out with, the greasy one. If Ivan is well enough to leave the hospital he's well enough to stay here on his own. I can drop in once in a while during my lunch break. Like every other Wednesday. Visiting homecare comes once a week. You're at work most of the time anyway. You'll hardly see him."

Renata turned to Carla. "We have to find the brighter side. Emma wants to be with Boris, I mean they love one another. You ought to see them together. It's like they … glow. Do you know what it feels like to glow, Carla?"

But Renata knew from this blank couldn't-care-less face that she was looking at a veteran who had stopped glowing a long time ago.

Carla said, "I'm overloaded with paperwork. I have the same caseload as last year but with reduced funding. I have to operate blindly with information that's usually wrong. All this I must accept. But I do not have to accept manipulation."

CHAPTER FORTY-TWO

Dr. Simpson was feeling like a teenager on his way to a first date, trying to think of what to talk about in advance. A haircut? He didn't need a haircut. But here he was, right on time for his haircut. The Cutting Corner was a narrow shop with floor-to-ceiling mirrors and three black leather beauty salon chairs; one, two, three, in a row, all empty. Renata was sitting at the back on a stool, next to shelves lined with beauty products. She pointed to the chair nearest the window. He settled back in the soft leather. In the mirror he watched Renata assemble her instruments: various scissors, combs, and a spray bottle. The tight jeans fit perfectly over every curve of her bottom, the black sweater over every curve of her top, and her blonde hair pulled back into a ponytail completed the image. A beautiful young woman.

But then in the stark overhead fluorescent lights, he noticed that the bluish tinge under her eye was more pronounced. "How is that bruise doing? Healing up okay?"

"Oh … well, yeah. What's the standard line? I walked into a door." She fastened the sheet around him and cranked up the chair a few inches. To make up for his short stature, he realized.

"How long ago was that?"

"About two weeks … Ivan's heart attack was on Wednesday, this was the day before, on Tuesday."

"It's taken all this time? Must have been some bruise."

He watched her in the mirror as she picked up the spray bottle and began to wet his hair. Renata's scissor hand was her right, he noticed, suspended now as the fingers of the left hand were busy at the back of his neck. She seemed to be trying to understand the hair pattern, which didn't make any sense because his hair was perfectly straight, not very thick, and totally boring. He had worn his hair the same way since high school, parted on the left, short on the sides, long on the top, a businessman cut for clinical confidence, not like some of the young doctors, some with shaved heads even.

He asked, "Why did he do it?"

At this question her left hand stopped exploring the back of his neck. She stared out the front window. Tears formed in the corner of each eye.

"Katria, my little sister, is terrified of him," she murmured. "Completely and utterly terrified. She's been … hospitalized."

Dr. Simpson thought, I shouldn't have asked the question. He said, "My hands are tied, Renata. His bed is needed. There are patients waiting in the hallways. But explain to me, why did he hit you?"

She met his eyes in the mirror.

"Could we talk alone please, Dr. Simpson?" She nodded to the front of the shop as the door swung open and two ladies appeared. They stood at the door, the one arranging time with the other for a pickup. The older lady entered and the other lady left, apparently mother and daughter. The mother took a seat to wait her turn.

"Of course," he switched the tone of his voice from clinical to empathetic. He had been working hard at the empathy part, not that he didn't have it. But he was a shy and studious man. Nose in a book. "Of course," he repeated softly. "…although I'm not too sure how far ahead I'm booked. That might be a problem."

"Waiting lists, I know. Like in the Soviet Union my nana would say, God rest her soul. Just a thought. But isn't there anything we could do now? Like a transfer to a long-term hospital or, you know, a private hospital, you know, keep him there for a while. Because it's going—" she broke into a sob — "to be too much for us."

He had already assured her that Ivan, at present at least, would not be abusing anyone. But he knew that a heart condition would not change an abusive personality. Even an invalid in a wheelchair can figure out new ways to be abusive.

She recovered. She returned to the cut.

"Emma's working things through. But she works twelve-hour days. There will be no one at home to look after him."

Dr. Simpson was wondering, What are my chances? She's in need of help and I'm in need of companionship. But no, I'm too old for her. Although, twentysomething women marry fortysomething men all the time, especially if that fortysomething man is a heart surgeon. But no. In my hospital and in my office, I'm a big man, but in fact everywhere else I'm a small man, and under this sheet I feel even smaller. Everyone must look smaller under her sheet. Whatever their status, doctor, lawyer, they must shrink away under Renata's sheet.

Dr Simpson tried to sit up straighter.

"I'm sorry, Doctor. You're here for a haircut, not to listen to my complaints."

"I have a bit of time. Renata. No need to rush it."

"Like the doctor shows on TV, the surgeon is always in a rush to return to the OR to do a few bypasses before going to a speaking engagement to raise money for bypass equipment."

"And for better homecare. I understand your problem, Renata."

She got busy with the scissors and the comb. Her long fingers were quick and precise. As she moved from the side to the back, he saw in the mirrors that the bluish tinge along her cheek, covered by makeup to hide the damage, looked a little more serious than she was admitting. He had signed the standard Wellness Assessment of the Caregiver, completed by Carla, who often had no choice but to check everything as okay, even when it wasn't. This was not Carla's fault. Government homecare was hopelessly underfunded, understaffed, and in general hopelessly hopeless.

He said, "I have a lunch meeting tomorrow but I might be able to skip that. I could meet you in the cafeteria."

She continued with the cut without answering.

Dr. Simpson felt her rejection and back tracked. "What I meant, if you needed to talk it through, just a suggestion…" He was thinking, *She's guessed I have intentions and is thinking up a polite "no thanks."*

She undid the cover and shook it out. "I'm booked solid tomorrow. Why don't you come to my house for dinner?" She shrugged. "Tomorrow evening maybe?"

Dr. Simpson didn't know what to say. His mind buzzed with rationalization. She was not his patient, not a hospital employee, she needed his help, the only time he could see her for a consultation was after hours, so there was no reason why he could not say yes.

She bent over to slide the cover under the counter. She said, "You've been looking at my bruise. Both eyes were black and blue. Every morning, I'd wake up thinking the swelling must be gone by now. Then I'd look in the mirror."

"But why did he hit you?"

"He'd been drinking, you know. He's Russian, Comrade Ivan, we call him."

Dr. Simpson wanted to reach over to run his finger along her cheekbone. He imagined his hand under her chin tilting her head to the light as he gently felt with soft fingertips the bridge of her nose. He reached up and ran his fingers through his new haircut, smoothing it down a little. "Dinner would be nice. Yes, that would be very nice."

CHAPTER FORTY-THREE

Dr. Simpson arrived at the door of Renata's apartment in a bit of a fluster. He should never have agreed to this dinner engagement. He was too nervous. If he wasn't talking medicine, he was uncomfortable, had nothing to say. And how do you talk to a hairdresser? And he had forgotten to bring something, like flowers or a bottle of wine or chocolates. Isn't that what you do? So he had stopped at the Quickie Market, scanned along the shelves and the coolers, and finally decided on a bag of tater tots.

He stood at Renata's door, gazing at the picture of the tater tots, thinking, This is ridiculous. He should go to the corner store he had passed on the way and at least pick up some kind of chocolates. But he was already late.

She opened the door.

"Sorry, I'm late. Ten minutes. Sorry." He handed her the tater tots. "Not much. Sorry. I was in a rush."

He sank down onto the edge of the living-room chesterfield. Renata, wearing a red blouse and faded jeans and high heels, settled down in the chair opposite.

"I got here as soon as I could. Things are piling up in the OR."

"Can you at least stay for dinner?"

"Of course, Renata. I've brought you some pamphlets. Homecare information." As he handed them to her, he glanced at the injured eye, noting that the bruise had gone.

"Stress is bad for you, Doctor. You need to relax a little bit. How about a drink? How about I mix you a Russian to have with your tater tots?"

He undid the buttons of his suit jacket. "No thank you, Renata. Maybe one later."

"How do things pile up in the OR, like sick people on hold in the halls, stacked like circling airplanes waiting to be landed?"

"Something like that. I've lost a day this week because I have court tomorrow."

Renata leaned forward, her eyes wide. "What did you do, Dr. Simpson? You killed somebody's granny on the gurney?"

He smiled. "Not at all. An autopsy report. A cold case file from years ago." He undid his tie.

"You testify about autopsy reports?"

"Sometimes, yes."

Renata studied his face, her expression somber, waiting for more information, it seemed. About her father probably. Well, who knows what she was waiting for.

She looked like a younger version of the girl who did the six o'clock news. She always seemed to be looking directly at him, except of course she was looking directly at everyone, while in fact, she was looking directly at no one. She always dressed in ultra-conservative, ultra-neutral clothes to encourage the viewer to think about world events and not about her. Renata was dressed as though she didn't want this viewer, Dr. Simpson, to think of world events. And the fix of those blue eyes staring straight at him was making him more nervous. He said, "Maybe a drink. That would be a good idea."

She got up. He could not help but watch her stop-the-clock hip action float her into the kitchen. That is the image she left him with as he listened to the fridge door open and close, open and close.

Renata handed him the drink, clear liquid with a slice of lemon on top. "Is something quick okay for dinner, Dr. Simpson? Like salad and cold ham? You can explain to me about the homecare while you drink your Russian. The salad and ham will be ready whenever you are."

"That will be fine. Thank you."

"Should I warm up the tater tots?"

"You don't eat them like chips?"

"I don't think so, Dr. Simpson. They're frozen."

"Oh, well, in such a hurry ... Please. And would you happen to have an ibuprofen, Renata? I have a headache."

"Come into the kitchen, I'll see."

He followed her into a small galley kitchen while she looked through a cupboard above the sink. She read the directions. "One ibuprofen with a glass of water and keep away from children. Do you have any children to keep away from, Dr. Simpson?"

"No, I don't."

"Oh my gosh! No children. How come?"

"I've never had time to, you know, go on dates, get married..."

"You'll be a good catch for some lucky girl."

"Oh, thank you, but ...why do you say that?"

"I don't know but I guess I don't see you as a normal male. I don't think you wear the same clothes for seven days in a row. You don't have a one-track mind about sex and beer. But I really can't say because we haven't hung out enough for me to know that. So maybe we should hang out more, get to know one another better. Know what I'm saying?"

Renata led the way back to the living room and set her glass on the coffee table along with two three-inch pickles on a plate. She slipped her hand inside her blouse and gently began to rub along her shoulder.

"Is that sore in there?" he asked. "The bruise is gone, I see, but anything else, cracked ribs or anything like that?"

"Nothing serious."

"Collarbone fractures are common; they can be very painful."

"I'll recover. Good Russian stock. Like that drink, Russian tradition. The reason they drank so much vodka in the war was because it was cheaper than milk or soda or water. But too many soldiers were ending up in comas from alcohol poisoning. So the Russian army gave the order to take it with lemon or pickle to neutralize the alcohol."

"Can I try it with the pickle?

"But you have to drink it properly. You stir the lemon around the glass with the finger and then, holding it to one side, down the hatch."

She showed him. "Try it."

"A bare finger? You don't wear latex gloves?"

"Latex gloves? To have a drink?"

"But you're inserting your finger."

"Oh yeah … I guess … But the vodka kills the germs."

"Germs are my area of expertise. An obsession, almost."

He studied the drink.

"I think you need to relax a little, Dr. Simpson. Just stick in the finger and give a stir and down the hatch and don't worry about the germs."

"A mighty creature is the germ," said Dr. Simpson.

"Don't you dare tell me you're going to wash your finger first."

"You want me to put my finger into my drink without first washing my finger?"

"Yeah … Totally. I do. So do it."

He studied the drink.

She put her hand on his. "Pretend the vodka is a germ slayer. In fact, look at it as an experiment. If you drink your drink and don't come down with something, that will mean the vodka slew the germs and you can use it in OR."

Dr. Simpson stared at his drink.

"One stir, doctor. We'll do it together."

They stirred the drinks.

"Then you lick off your finger like this." She stuck her finger into her mouth and quick pulled it out. "Like that."

He studied his finger, now glistening with drops of vodka.

"Don't be a sissy."

He inserted his finger.

"Good boy. Now one stir. Like this." She took his hand. "One stir like this, hold the finger — like this — and down the hatch."

He pinned the lemon against the glass and raised it to his mouth and drank half without spilling.

"Way to go! You're a natural. You know why? You've got long fingers and they're used to doing precise stuff, like cutting people open and sticking in your finger. Finish it off."

Dr. Simpson finished it off. He licked his finger. He checked his watch and waited.

"Do you feel a sickness on your horizon from all those germs, Dr. Simpson? Should I call 911?"

"Three minutes," he said. "Alcohol takes three minutes to go from the stomach to the brain. I'm more relaxed already."

"Straight to the ticker." Renata smiled, and her blue eyes sparkled. "I have never in my life seen anyone who could do a Russian the first time. But maybe it was a fluke. Let me see you do it again."

"No thank you, Renata. One is enough. I have a court case tomorrow."

"No problem. You won't have a hangover if you eat a pickle. Sailor's Dills. Imported from Russia." She inserted the pickle into her mouth and, her lips pouting into a pucker, drew it in and out, playing with it before taking the first bite. "Yum yum. Crispy-edged, like a good pickle."

She poured him another shot and laid out another pickle, and she poured herself another shot and laid out a pickle beside the other pickle. "That's your pickle, this is my pickle. You first."

He picked up the glass and downed it in one gulp.

"Ahh, perfect. Now the pickle."

He took a bite of the pickle.

She picked up her glass and downed the drink and picked up her pickle and began to play with it with her tongue.

"Better than coffee and doughnuts," he said, his head now drifting and, from watching the in and out of her tongue with her pickle, his own was beginning to think about it.

She said, "So you're not married." When she slid a little closer, he could smell her shampoo and what must have been a touch of perfume added during one of her trips to the kitchen. She continued to suck on her pickle. She said, "Here. Have a bite from my pickle."

"Uhhh, Renata."

"Don't be a sissy."

He bit from the pickle she had been sucking on.

"Now I bite from your pickle."

He picked up his pickle and inserted it into her mouth and she took a bite. He said, "I want to do the lemon one again. As an experiment."

She made the drinks. "We do it together, stir the lemon, down the hatch, then lick the finger."

They did it together, down the hatch, not as smooth as Renata but pretty good.

She held out her finger. "Now you lick my finger."

He leaned in close and stuck out his tongue.

"Not like that. You take it right in your mouth"

He hesitated.

"What a disappointment. All those germs waiting on my finger, getting ready for the journey into your mouth and down your throat and into your bloodstream, like promising them a big adventure and then you change your mind."

When he moved close enough to take the extended finger into his mouth, he could identify the perfume, fragrance of lilac or lily of the valley. Definitely lily of the valley.

"Suck off the vodka."

He sucked off the vodka.

"Now me."

He put his finger into her mouth and she worked it with her tongue. Already Dr. Simpson was feeling more than relaxed. He made a mental note: On an empty stomach, nothing since breakfast, the liquor in seconds speeds from stomach to bloodstream, and then straight to the brain.

She fixed two more. "Aunt Gizla drank her Russians with Dr. Goldstein, her goldfish. God bless her soul, may she rest in peace. And Dr. Goldstein. May he rest in peace." She wiped at her eye. "I changed his water. I bought him those, like, plastic seaweeds, you know, and little plastic coral thingies. Aunt Gizla liked animals and didn't like my dad poisoning everything. Rats and mice and raccoons and skunks."

Until this second, Dr. Simpson was only vaguely aware that, as the vodka had sped from stomach to bloodstream to brain, a shift of his body closer to Renata's had caused her blouse to go from one button buttoned to unbuttoned to two buttons buttoned to unbuttoned.

Renata didn't seem to notice. "Down the hatch. Let's drink to Aunt Gizla and Dr. Goldstein."

This Russian had barely landed in his stomach before launching itself directly into his pickle and sending Dr. Simpson in the direction of the lily of the valley. But he pulled himself upright and got control of himself. He reached up to straighten his tie. He was not wearing a tie.

"My aunt and nana were heavy vodka drinkers, the Russian tradition, with the finger. Both of them." She wiped at her eye. "And now they're gone. So sad."

"Renata, do you mind if I … I'd like to clarify a few things."

"Of course," she said. "What's up? Is that a pickle in your pocket or do you love me? Just kidding. But yeah, go ahead. What's up?"

"Let me be honest with you. I was interviewed by a detective…"

She looked straight at him with a blue-eyed startled stare. "A detective? Why? You killed someone's granny?"

"Routine, I think. Did your nana and aunt have a particular pattern for their drinking, like before lunch, first thing in the morning, something like that?"

"Five o'clock in the afternoon."

"On an empty stomach?"

"Yes. They were both rigid personalities, same thing every day, no snack, no cake in the afternoon, one light lunch, dinner at six, that was the routine."

"So how many vodkas would they have?"

"Three, four, five, doubles, down the hatch."

"So they would ingest about what, eight ounces of vodka in quick order."

"Yes. Why?"

"I'm noticing how quickly the alcohol goes from the stomach to the bloodstream. And then bam. Straight to the heart."

"Quick, yeah, I guess. Totally."

"Alcohol can contribute to the likelihood of heart failure, especially in older women."

"No kidding!"

"Your father works with rodent control poison. He washes his hands after he handles the poison?"

"He probably can't. He's on the road, works out of his van. But I think he carries a toothbrush. He was a no-cavities freak."

"He brushes his teeth with hands that handle poison?"

"He eats his lunch first."

"Toothbrushes are full of germs, Renata."

"He should keep his toothbrush in a glass of vodka."

"Well … disinfectant of some sort."

"He'd come home from work after poisoning rats all day, straight to the refrigerator for his vodka without ever washing his hands once. I'd say to him, 'Don't you think you should wash your hands after handling all that poison?'"

"In the OR I scrub my hands, arms, face. No germs. But then I'm a cardiologist."

"You should scrub your hands with vodka.'

"And as a cardiologist I should have known how quickly alcohol travels into the bloodstream and — bam — into the heart. This is astonishing."

She got up and made two more.

"Does it smell?" she asked, returning with the drinks.

"Does what smell?"

"When you cut someone open. Is that what happened to the granny?"

"Like raw steak. Unless there's infection."

"From germs."

"Yes, from germs."

"Tell me something, Doctor. When you examine a young woman on your table, does her body, you know, imprint on your mind, and then bam into your heart and then do you go home and fantasize about her? And don't say no because I'll know you're lying."

"There's always a nurse in the room, Renata."

"So if I was lying naked on your table and you examined me and then I got up and went home, you wouldn't think about me after I was gone."

"Only if I discovered something wrong."

"And then you would call me for a follow-up exam?"

"Yes. I would."

"Sounds like a free peep show."

"It's not free. I get paid for doing it."

"Yeah … totally. I see what you mean. But this sore shoulder, Doctor. When I move my arm like this, I get a pain along here. Could you examine it for me? For free?"

"Not without a nurse present."

Renata frowned. "I don't get it. If I was lying in a roadside ditch, you wouldn't examine me if there was no nurse present?"

"Of course I would. A life-and-death situation."

"If I came into your office and said I have a shoulder ache you'd examine me."

"No, I wouldn't. I'm a cardiologist."

"What if I act as your nurse and you act as a shoulder doctor and you examine my shoulder?" Renata stood up. "The nurse stands here keeping watch; I lie back and you examine me." She flopped down on the couch, legs outstretched. "But you have to wash your hands first."

He stared at his hands. "I'll use the finger I stuck in the vodka."

"Your finger? What kind of exam is this?"

"Your shoulder, you said."

"Breast bone, you're hoping. And don't say no because then I'll know you're lying. How about another vodka to make sure that finger has no germs?"

Renata got up to get the vodka. Dr. Simpson settled into the soft cushions of the couch and stretched out his legs. He removed his shoes and placed them at the end of the couch, out of the way. He closed his eyes and thought about how Ivan Boscov, handler of rat poisons, drank Russian vodkas. Russia, like many European countries, didn't have the hygiene concerns of this country. Over the years, rat poison on his fingers, under his fingernails, entered his mouth as the result of poor hygiene habits to gradually build up to potentially lethal doses in his liver and kidneys. The two older Boscovs, sister and mother, knocking back the vodka every day at five o'clock. Hmmm.

Renata returned with the vodka and sat beside him. The glass was sweating from the cold tonic. He hadn't noticed the other three glasses had been sweating. The room was warmer now, he thought, getting up to remove his suit jacket.

Renata said, "In Russia, two people drinking together after they stir and down the hatch and suck the finger and bite the pickle, if it's a guy and girl, or, you know, good friends, that becomes a bonding sort of, like exchanging friendship rings, and they exchange kisses."

This was a miracle. This beautiful young woman, Renata, by some mysterious hand dropped out of the sky, was now talking about kissing and bonding.

"You don't have to stick your finger in your vodka to examine me, Dr. Simpson. I was just kidding. I'm sure your finger is clean. But then I don't think about germs much, hardly ever. But in your line of work, you must have to think about them constantly."

"Constantly."

He stuck his finger into his vodka and drew it out and she took the finger and stuck it into her mouth and she curled her tongue around it.

"This is like trading sucks. You suck mine and I suck yours. Did you do this when you were little, with candy, I mean? I bet you did.

That's why you've got this germs obsession. Kids making you trade sucks. When I was little, about five, I wanted to be a nurse. I'd dress up like a nurse. I didn't want to operate on people. I wanted to feed people. Sometimes the boy next door came over to play and I made him lie on the floor and I'd feed him. Lie on the floor and I'll show you."

Dr. Simpson hesitated. "Uhhh … Renata…"

"I'd lie him on the floor and cover him with a blanket and feed him his tater tots so isn't it amazing that you brought me tater tots? It's not coincidence, you know. It's synchronicity, a moment in time when, between two people, boundaries disappear and tater tots appear."

"Did this boy like tater tots?"

"I never asked him. I was the nurse. He had to do what I said. So lie on the floor, Dr. Simpson. Don't be a sissy. The tater tots are ready. They're like little potatoes, my mother made them. I know, I know. They're not good for your heart. Straight to the coffin. But do you know what, Doctor? These come from Russia. It says so on the package. During the war, all they had to eat was tater tots."

He picked one up between thumb and finger and studied it, a round ball the size of a chocolate, covered with breading.

"It's a good thing you're not married, Doctor. Your wife would feed you rat poison."

"Why?"

"You're too fussy — germs, latex gloves. You look like you're about to eat a snail."

He popped it into his mouth and chewed slowly.

"Good," he said. "Quite tasty."

"Quite, yeah totally. Have another. See how long the breading takes to get to your heart. You could wire yourself up to a monitor and measure blood pressure and beats and stuff. Swellings too."

"Swellings?"

"Just kidding. Seeing if you were paying attention. Which I see that you are."

"You do dress provocatively, Renata. And you certainly smell good."

"That little boy I told you about a minute ago, he'd come through the door and lay down on the floor for me to feed him his tater tots and bam straight away his heart pumped his blood into his … Do you want to know how I could tell? I'll show you."

Renata disappeared into the bedroom and returned with a blanket, which she spread out on the floor.

"Renata, this is…"

"If a five-year-old boy can do it … Well, that was a lie. I think he was fifteen. But he wasn't a sissy. So lie down, you're looking a bit unsteady. Let me help — oops, down you go, Dr. Simpson, before you tip the canoe."

CHAPTER FORTY-FOUR

She attracted no attention as she hurried off the elevator, along a busy hallway, and into Comrade Ivan's room. He was lying on his back, hands at his sides, sound asleep, his skin as pale as the pillow. He looked like he was already dead. He looked like he'd been left there by the maggots who wanted nothing to do with the killer of all things crawling.

No such luck. She could tell by the heaviness of his breathing. But she knew from the lifeless expression on his face that he was heavily out of it.

"Time for a change of pillow," she whispered, shaking him a little.

When he didn't stir, she slipped her hand under his neck and tried to pull out the pillow, but only got it partway. When he came to and grunted, she said, "It's the nurse, come to change your pillow."

She was about to give it a good pull when two ladies came into the room.

"This isn't Mr. Eventree," said the first lady. "We're in the wrong room."

The second lady, who had come closer to peer down. "What's wrong with this poor man?"

"Uh, heart attack."

They left.

The visit from the two ladies unnerved her. She decided she should come back later when visiting hours were over. Back in the hallway she paid attention to the set-up, something she should have done when she first got there: the nurses' station at one end, two washrooms partway along, only two doors away from his room.

In the ladies' washroom, she sat on the toilet and waited. She stayed in there until just before visiting hours ended. But there were still too many people passing in the hall. She settled down in a cubicle in the washroom to wait. After almost an hour she opened the door to peek out. It was nine-fifteen by the hall clock. Everything was quiet. She thought she'd wait another half hour. She settled back in the cubicle and waited. She leaned forward, her head in her hands until, certain all the visitors were gone, she cracked the door. Because only the night light shone in the corridor, she could not at first see all the way to the nurses' station. She opened the door a little wider and glanced down the hall. The nurses would almost certainly be sitting at the desk, she thought, but from this position she could see only the corner of the counter. Uncertain what to do, she slipped back into the washroom. She heard the phone ring and heard a nurse answer. She could not hear what was said, but because she heard laughter she decided it must be a personal call, which meant the nurse would not be paying attention to any of the rooms or the hallway. It's now or never, she thought, opening the door and stepping out. She reached Ivan's door in a few seconds and slipped in unseen. The laughter at the nurse's station continued.

He was still lying on his back, his arms at his sides. She pulled the pillow out from underneath his head and was about to bring it down over his face when she realized that he was breathing so loudly the nurse might hear when he stopped. But this is nonsense, she thought. The nurse is too far up the hallway. But perhaps she should shut the door. But, she reasoned, a shut door would arouse suspicion to anyone passing by. But, she thought, if someone came by and looked in, crouched down at the far side of the bed she'd be hidden. But, she realized, unless she stood right over top of him, she'd not be able to hold the pillow over his face.

Suddenly, Ivan stirred in his sleep, his nose twitched, and he raised his right hand to scratch it. Then he scratched his cheek and forehead.

She stood at the door, listening to the muffled voice of the nurse at the station. Because the elevator was right across the from the nurses' station, she'd have to use the stairs at the end of the hall. She had to do it now while the hall was empty. She climbed onto the bed and sat on his chest. As she leaned all her weight into the pillow she was surprised at the feebleness of his struggles. Only his right arm had enough strength to raise itself off the bed. She put the pillow back under his head, and without looking back, walked down the hall toward the exit. At the open door, one quick glance over her shoulder told her the hallway was empty, and by the sound of the low muffled laughter, the nurse was still on the phone. Well, she thought, she'll be busy for a few minutes and in a few minutes, I'll be guaranteed gone, and so will he.

No one paid her any attention as she hurried across the lobby. In such a rush, she didn't see the man in blue scrubs. She bumped right into him. Her purse, knocked from her hand, spilled out onto the floor and came to rest against one wall. The man picked up her wallet that lay open at his feet.

"I'm sorry," she apologized.

"Quite all right." He handed over her wallet.

"I was seeing my father…" She knelt down to retrieve her blue eye shadow which lay next to her purse. She snatched both up and put the eye shadow away. Then she noticed her driver's license which had slid across the floor to rest under an empty wheelchair. She grabbed it up and jammed it into her purse.

When she turned to face the doctor, she could not believe her eyes. He was halfway down the hall, walking quickly away, disappearing through the swinging doors. As she headed for the main exit doors, she noticed a long line of framed pictures hanging on the wall. She had to double check. She went over to look more closely, running her eyes from one picture to the next to the next, checking the name of each resident doctor. Her eye stopped on the picture of a man with hair that was darker, with a smile that made him look less serious, but definitely the man she had run into: Dr. Simpson.

CHAPTER FORTY-FIVE

Miss Little came in and put her arm around Katria's shoulder. "Katria. Your father. We got a call from Emma. He has passed away."

She hugged Katria.

"Death is hard to understand when you're young. I like to think of it as he's stepped into the next room; out of sight, but not out of mind. Cherish the good memories you have of your father, Katria. And of your aunt Gizla, and of your nana."

...

Katria was sitting next to Dominic, who was rocking on the floor, sending messages to the snack lady to bring Katria an extra sandwich and a piece of apple pie. Sure enough, when the elevator door opened, it was the cafeteria lady bringing Katria an extra sandwich and there, on a separate plate, a piece of apple pie.

Snacks for everyone else arrived ten minutes later on a trolley. Dominic reached out with two big paws for his glass of milk and tipped his head back and drank it in one gulp. He set the empty glass on the table and belched. Katria picked up her sandwich and her pie and detoured through the lounge, and returned to her room, a student nurse following to make certain she ate everything. The student didn't look much older than Katria. She was dressed in ordinary street clothes, jeans and top, plain-looking, like a student.

Katria said, "I want to be alone."

"What for?"

"To think about my father."

"You can think to yourself about your father while you're eating your sandwich. I won't say anything while you're thinking."

"They lock my bathroom door. If I want to go I have to ask and then the nurse stands outside the door to listen."

"You must feel trapped," said the student.

"If I was an animal, I could chew my leg off."

"You could, yes."

"But I don't want to. I want to get better."

Katria finished one sandwich and took the second.

"What's your name?"

"Kelly, almost the same as yours."

...

"Renata mentioned it was a nice funeral," said Dr. Enright.

Katria crossed her legs and sat up straight. She wished she was wearing that sleeveless casual hippie dress Moms always wore for her doctor appointments. Katria said, "Moms took a video of him on her cellphone the day he arrived in the cemetery and sent it to me. He looks sort of dried up and walks like in the *Undead* movies, sort of lurching."

"So who poisoned him?"

"Mom's said when the police came and asked him that question, his face kind of boiled up red trying to find the words. So, the policeman gave him a pencil and a piece of paper to write it on."

"So who poisoned him?" asked Dr. Enright.

"Moms said the policeman didn't say it like that. He said, 'Who did this to you' and gave him the pencil and paper."

"And what did he write?"

"Not write. Print. Which reminds me…"

Katria handed Dr. Enright a sheet of paper. "Moms recited a poem to Dominic and he wrote it down and gave it to me."

Dr. Enright read it out loud:

The wool arrives in boxes

She orders from Mary Carol,

Like one of Mary Carol's spiders,

She examines each thread in a row

To make sure the order is right

Before setting her fingers to work,

clickety-clack, clickety-clack,

I'm going to get them back.

Thousands of angry knots,

Thousands of angry stitches,

The knitter's hands slide back and forth

Her jaw grinds in angry twitches

As each finger knits identical stitches

From each of the two angry bitches.

But now they've set aside their needles,

Curled black fingernails into their lap

So soon their loops will unravel.

Clackety Click. Clickety Clack.

I finally got them back.

Dr. Enright leaned back in his chair "So who is the poisoner?"

"Do you know what, Dr. Enright? When I look out the hospital window, I can see my mother's grave even though it's on the other side of the city. I never used to think about cemeteries, except when I was with my dad, how upset he got if a funeral procession with all the cars with the little black flags like a parade was going through the red light. His face would boil up red and he'd get out of his white van and shout at the funeral, 'It's green, I should be able to go.'"

Katria unfolded her legs and slid down in her chair until she was almost horizontal, her hands laced across her stomach. "I used to sit like this when I wasn't eating because I had lost so much weight I thought I'd blow away. In the subway, so the train wouldn't blow me away before I could jump in front of it, I crouched behind the newspaper box. And do you know what, Dr. Enright? While I was sitting behind the newspaper box on the subway platform, I felt a glimmer of life come from the tunnel and stand next to me. My mother sat down beside me and took my hand. It was in my pocket, and she took it out, and she said, 'Hands, Katria, are like feet. There is a left and a right. But unlike feet, hands are magical. They are capable of knitting, yes. But they are also capable of holding and helping and leading and healing and protecting. I know, Katria, you can't believe in words, but maybe you can begin to believe in hands.'"

"Ah, yes. Beautiful. And then what happened?"

"Moms brought me here for something to eat. She said I needed to put some meat on my bones. She's Scottish. 'Put some meat on your bones.'"

"Ah," Dr. Enright placed his elbows on the desk and clasped his hands in a steeple. "I love it. The essence of what is becomes the substance of what's not seen. That is why they call this place the Cathedral."

Katria sat up and crossed one leg over her knee and leaned a little forward. She ran her fingers through her hair. "Do you like my hair, Dr. Enright?"

"Very fetching."

She settled further into her chair and wrapped her hospital robe around herself. She sat back in her chair, then slid down again on her spine, her legs stretched out in front of her.

Dr. Enright said, "So, as I understand it, the afternoon before your father died, the detective asked him who poisoned him. What did he say?"

"He couldn't talk. Remember? I told you. So the detective gave him a pad and a pencil."

"Yes. And what did he write?"

"Not write. Print."

"Print. Of course. What did he print?"

"S A R A. He spelled it wrong. Moms spells her name 'Sarah.'"

END

www.ingramcontent.com/pod-product-compliance
Lightning Source LLC
Chambersburg PA
CBHW032116020726
47494CB00007BA/2099